Adam Morgan was every woman's ultimate dream...every wedding planner's financial fantasy!

Meredith reached into her portfolio and pulled out an assortment of wedding invitation samples and cake photos, spreading them out on the leather desktop. "These are just samples, of course. I have others, if none meet your needs."

What would meet Adam's needs, or rather *who*, was seated right in front of him. Meredith Baxter, with her bow-shaped, kissable mouth and figure that conjured up erotic thoughts, was an incredibly sexy woman.

"You're frowning, Mr. Morgan. Is something the matter?"

Pushing the material back to her, he shook his head. "Just use your own judgment, Miss Baxter. The only requirement I have is that the date be set and the invitations printed immediately."

"But you don't have a bride—"

"No buts about it, Miss Baxter. Plan the wedding... as if it were your own."

"Millie Criswell rules *when it comes to humor and passion. Don't miss* The Wedding Planner!"
—Bestselling Silhouette Desire author
Leanne Banks

Dear Reader,

Welcome to another month of wonderful books from Harlequin American Romance! We've rounded up the best stories by your favorite authors, with the hope that you will enjoy reading them as much as we enjoy bringing them to you.

Kick-start a relaxing weekend with the continuation of our fabulous miniseries, THE DADDY CLUB. The hero of Mindy Neff's *A Pregnancy and a Proposal* is one romantic daddy who knows how to sweep a woman off her feet!

Beloved historical author Millie Criswell makes her contemporary romance debut with *The Wedding Planner*. We are thrilled to bring you this compelling story of a wealthy bachelor out to find himself a bride...with a little help from the wedding consultant who wishes she were his only choice!

We've also got the best surprises and secrets. Bailey Dixon has a double surprise for Michael Wade in Tina Leonard's delightful new Western, *Cowboy Be Mine*. And in Bonnie K. Winn's *The Mommy Makeover*, a dedicated career woman is suddenly longing for marriage—what *is* her handsome groom's secret?

With best wishes for happy reading from Harlequin American Romance...

Melissa Jeglinski
Associate Senior Editor

The Wedding Planner

MILLIE CRISWELL

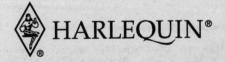

HARLEQUIN®

TORONTO • NEW YORK • LONDON
AMSTERDAM • PARIS • SYDNEY • HAMBURG
STOCKHOLM • ATHENS • TOKYO • MILAN • MADRID
PRAGUE • WARSAW • BUDAPEST • AUCKLAND

ISBN 0-373-16810-1

THE WEDDING PLANNER

Visit us at www.romance.net

Printed in U.S.A.

ABOUT THE AUTHOR

Millie Criswell is a national bestselling author and winner of the *Romantic Times Magazine* Career Achievement Award and the Reviewer's Choice Award. She's published more than a dozen historical romance novels, but is making her contemporary category romance debut with Harlequin American Romance. Millie lives in Virginia with her husband and her neurotic but loving Boston terrier. Her daughter is a practicing attorney in Florida and her son attends law school at West Virginia University.

Don't miss the historical prequel to this novel, *The Marrying Man*, available April 2000 from Harlequin Historicals.

Chapter One

Adam Morgan was certifiable, totally irrational and just plain-old nuts.

Money couldn't buy happiness. Well, it obviously couldn't buy sanity, either. For all his money, good looks and breeding, the man seated across the round mahogany table from Meredith, looking so earnest in his two-thousand-dollar Armani suit and three-hundred-dollar white shirt, while he tossed sunflower seed remains all over her new carpet, was a few slices short of a two-dollar loaf of white bread.

She continued to stare at him in disbelief, wondering if she'd heard him correctly. When he repeated himself, there was no doubt in her mind that a large vacuum existed between those well-shaped ears.

"I need a wife, Miss Baxter. I'd like you to find me one as soon as possible. I'm on a tight deadline, and I'm willing to pay handsomely for your effort." He cracked another sunflower seed between his flashing white, oh-so-very-straight teeth. It was obvious he flossed regularly. Another reason to dislike him.

Gazing at the checkbook now being waved in her direction, her toe started tapping against the mauve carpeting. When nervous, some people chewed their nails, toyed with the ends of their hair or gnawed the inside of their cheek. Meredith tapped. In fact, she was tapping so fast at the moment she could probably qualify for a job at Radio City dancing with the Rockettes. Her right knee knocked against the underbelly of the table, and she pressed it with her palm to stop the motion.

She was an excellent wedding planner and took pride in making her customers' special day the most perfect it could be. But she wasn't a magician or a marriage broker.

Adam Morgan didn't need a wife. He needed a shrink. And with his millions, he could afford the best psychiatrist Morgantown had to offer.

"Perhaps you don't understand what it is I do, Mr. Morgan. I'm a wedding consultant, not a matchmaker. Best Laid Plans will be happy to arrange for a church, rent a banquet hall for the reception, take care of the flowers, music and catering. But we don't enter into bridal selection—unless, of course, you're talking about bridal gowns. Those we can find."

Flicking an imaginary speck of dust off his expertly tailored navy-blue jacket, Adam Morgan drummed manicured fingers on the table. Everything about the man was manicured, from his perfectly coifed dark, wavy hair, to his highly polished cordovan wing tips. Meredith was pretty certain that if she were to take a peek at his boxers, there would be a crease in the silk material. He was definitely the silk-boxer type.

"Is there a problem with my attire, Miss Baxter? You keep staring at my lap." Adam's brow lifted, as if in challenge, though his expression remained bland. He suppressed the urge to laugh at the woman's obvious embarrassment. With her red hair and milky complexion, he suspected the lovely Miss Baxter couldn't hide much of what she was thinking. And what she was apparently thinking at the moment was quite intriguing. If his situation wasn't quite so dire, he'd be tempted to investigate further.

"Ah, no. There's no problem." Hoping her face wasn't the color of a cooked lobster—she hated her fair complexion—Meredith entwined her fingers and set them before her, trying to look businesslike, and doing her damnedest to keep her disappointment from showing.

When Morgan had strolled into her store thirty minutes before, she had recognized him immediately. His photo was constantly in the newspaper, either in the business pages or society section. When he'd announced that he wanted her to plan his wedding—a rather extravagant affair for a thousand people—she'd nearly passed out. The dollar signs flashing behind her eyelids had rendered her dizzy. But when he'd added the crazy stipulation about the bride… Well, she knew he was having a good laugh at her expense. Because if it wasn't a joke, than it meant that Adam Morgan, heir to the Morgan Coal Mining and Manufacturing fortune, was a deranged lunatic. The pile of seeds on her carpet was growing, making that seem a likely possibility.

The wealthy bachelor didn't bother to hide his frustration. The adoption deadline was closing in on him, and he didn't have the time to explain his motives, nor was he in the habit of doing so. Most who worked for Adam followed his instructions to the letter. Obviously the redhead had a mind of her own.

"I am well aware of the functions of a wedding planner, Miss Baxter. I came to you because my time is extremely limited. I have three months to find a bride, plan a wedding and get married. Which is why I'm willing to pay you a considerable amount of money for your trouble. I realize that finding a bridal candidate is not in your usual job description, and you will be compensated accordingly."

Meredith's greedy little heart was beating faster than a KitchenAid mixer. Money really was the root of all evil, and she could certainly use some. And, well, even if Morgan was a little bit nuts, what harm could it do? After all, it was his money, his decision, if he wanted to buy himself a wife. All she had to do was find the unfortunate female.

Answer: If she pulled off Morgan's wedding, which was sure to be *the* wedding of the decade, she'd have more business than she could handle.

Society types tended to follow each other's lead like sheep. Trends were set, fashion dictated and accepted, because they didn't have the guts to exert their individuality.

Except for Adam Morgan. Planning a wedding without a bride was definitely a novel idea.

"I assume you have some criteria for your future bride," she asked, unable to believe she was actually discussing the possibility with him. Now who was nuts?

Reaching into his inside coat pocket, the fastidious businessman extracted an envelope and placed it on the table, pushing it toward her. "Here's a list I've put together. Intelligence being the most important quality, of course."

Meredith's green eyes widened. She would have

guessed big breasts. Wealthy men like Adam Morgan usually went for flash not substance. Trophy wives. Although he probably wasn't old enough to have a sweet young thing dripping from his arm. She guessed him to be about thirty-four or -five. He needed another ten, fifteen years for that.

Meredith had read in the newspaper about his struggle to adopt his dead sister's two children. Marriage was probably a stipulation of the adoption procedure. Single parents were not usually successful candidates. After studying Adam Morgan, it was easy to see why he needed a wife to bring some normalcy to the proceedings.

"Do you make it a habit to woolgather, Miss Baxter?" Her cheeks blossomed again, and Adam swallowed his smile. Meredith Baxter would never win a game of strip poker.

Glancing at his gold Rolex, he frowned at the likely possibility that he was going to be late. He never allowed himself to be late for an engagement. Punctuality was the mark of an organized mind. "I have an appointment with my attorney in twenty-five minutes. I'm afraid I need an answer or I shall be forced to go to your competitor."

She looked into eyes as gray as the rain-laden clouds outside, at the long fingers toying with the red Windsor knot at his throat, at the impressive width of his shoulders, the swarthy tint to his complexion, and she wondered if he was as businesslike and controlling in bed.

"Miss Baxter?"

Meredith forced her attention back, then smiled, somewhat hesitantly. "Though your request is unusual and not something I'm usually confronted with—most grooms already have a bride when they come to me—I accept the job, Mr. Morgan. I require a deposit of ten thousand dollars, due to the magnitude of the wedding you have in mind.'' And due to the stack of old bills she'd yet to pay.

"Excellent.'' Without batting an eyelash or breaking a smile, he wrote out the check, scribbled his signature, which was totally illegible, and stood, handing it to her. "Be at my house at ten o'clock tomorrow morning, and we'll get started on the media coverage.''

Her eyes widened, and her voice grew small. "Media coverage?''

"The quickest way to find a bride, Miss Baxter, is to use the media. Once the story gets out that I'm looking for a bride, the newspapers and television stations will be only too happy to aid us in our search. I intend to use them shamelessly. As will you.''

"I will?'' She swallowed with some trepidation.

"You're darn right, you will. Those vultures have hounded and exploited my family for years. I think some payback is in order. And I am very good at paying back, make no mistake about that.''

The feral glint in his eyes made Meredith a believer. Adam Morgan was a man used to getting his own way.

"Weddings are supposed to be joyous occasions, Mr. Morgan. Some people wait their whole lives to find the right person, fall in love and get married. Are you sure you've thought this through? I mean— what about love?''

He didn't bother to hide his disdain at the question or at her impertinence in asking it. "You're beginning to sound like a poorly written romance novel, Miss Baxter.''

She stiffened, her chin lifting a notch. ''I happen to love romance novels, Mr. Morgan.''

He started to say something—sarcastic, no doubt!—then thought better of it and said instead, ''I'm not the romantic type. I don't have time for hearts and flowers and happily ever after. In my opinion what I'm doing can be likened to a business merger. Two sides with similar views and interests coming together to form a successful union for the good of the company or, in this case, the good of the family unit.''

''So, in the immortal words of Tina Turner— 'What's Love Got To Do with It?' I think I understand.'' The man was cold, heartless. She pitied the poor woman who was foolish enough to marry him.

He looked at her strangely. ''Who is Tina Turner?''

Meredith held out her hand. ''An old family friend, Mr. Morgan. Don't worry about a thing. Your upcoming nuptials are in excellent hands.''

Gazing down at those excellent hands, he said before releasing hers, ''Your polish is chipped, Miss Baxter. And you have a run in your left stocking.''

Her mouth dropped open at the man's audacity, her eyes clouding in anger, and she didn't notice how the corners of his mouth had tilted. ''Thank you very much, cretin, Neanderthal, arrogant meathead,'' she said between gritted teeth, but he was already out the door and didn't hear her.

''Anyone I know, sweetie?'' her assistant, Randall, asked, emerging from the back room in time to catch a glimpse of the man through the plate-glass window.

He'd just returned from delivering six candelabras to the First Baptist Church, where the Sanders wedding would take place on Saturday morning.

Meredith forced down her anger. "Adam Morgan, our new client." She explained the details of the unorthodox wedding arrangement and the man's obnoxious observations, making Randall grin.

With his bleached-blond hair, tanned complexion, and brilliant blue eyes, Randall Cosby looked like a California beach boy. He was slight of build, but muscular, and had no difficulty performing the arduous tasks of lifting and hauling necessary to his position. He worked for Meredith part-time while attending law classes at West Virginia University.

"The man's obviously got good taste in women."

"What do you mean?"

"If he noticed the run in your stocking, sweetie, then he was staring at your legs. And your legs are one of your best features." He looked down at his own and pulled a face. "Mine are just too skinny and straight. No curvature at all to them. I've been cursed with brains and no body."

Meredith laughed. One of the things she liked best about Randall was his honesty. He was going to make a wonderful lawyer. "Thank you, I think. But I don't believe Mr. Morgan was looking at my legs for any reason other than to find fault. He's a stickler for details. And he's going to be a royal pain in the butt to work with."

Randall began straightening the bridal magazines on the long glass display counter. "Handsome, though. From what I saw of him, he's a very good-looking man, and quite a natty dresser." Randall was into clothing in a big way.

"Yes, he is that," Meredith agreed, a sigh escaping her lips. "But he's too arrogant and structured to suit me. I prefer someone a bit more animated. Adam Morgan is definitely not my type."

Randall arched a disbelieving brow. "Mickey Mouse, he's not." He shook his head. "Sweetie, you are way too picky. I used to think I was choosy, but you are much worse. I don't think there's a man alive who could live up to your expectations. The Prince Charmings of the world are few and far between. You're going to have to settle for a mere mortal if we're ever going to plan one of these fabulous weddings for you."

"I'm not in any rush to get married." She intended to wait for her knight in shining armor, no matter how long it took. There was someone special out there for her; she just knew it.

"Well, your mother is. Last time I visited Louise at the nursing home—we shared the loveliest boxed lunch from Grabber's Deli—she asked if you and I were dating. I told her that you weren't my type." He rolled his eyes, making Meredith laugh again.

"Mom's worried she's going to die before I can produce grandchildren for her to dote on. She's always trying to fix me up with the male nurses who work at Pleasant Acres. I guess she doesn't think I can get a date."

"She worries about you, sweetie. We all do."

Meredith smiled at her employee. "That's good, because that leaves me to worry about more important things. Speaking of which, we'd better get back to work. I've got to prepare myself for my meeting with Morgan tomorrow. I'm bearding the lion at ten."

He arched a brow. "Hmm. Sounds interesting."

"*Interesting* isn't the word for it, Randall. *Nauseating, aggravating,* but definitely not *interesting.*"

ATTORNEY PETER WEBBER leaned back in his tufted, red-leather swivel chair and noted the unusually high color on Adam Morgan's cheeks. As his lawyer for the past ten years, and best friend long before that, Peter was quite attuned to the man's shifting and often foul moods. Adam was displeased or distracted about something, and he would no doubt let him know soon enough what it was that was bothering him.

"As you suggested, I hired the wedding planner. We'll be meeting tomorrow morning to iron out the specifics of the upcoming wedding."

"What's he like?" Peter began making notes on a yellow legal pad. Adam was a stickler for recording even the most mundane details of every conversation.

"He is a she. Meredith Baxter from Best Laid Plans."

"Cute."

"She's attractive enough, I guess." Adam had always been intrigued by redheads. And she had the best-looking legs he'd seen in a very long time. Well-defined calves, shapely ankles. He adored the way her cheeks filled with color whenever she became embarrassed, which, judging by what he'd already observed, was often.

"I meant the name of her business."

"Oh."

Adam squirmed restlessly in his seat, and Peter swallowed his smile. He hadn't seen the man this distracted in a while. "What does Miss Baxter think of your plan to wed?"

"From the peculiar way she was staring at me, my guess is she thinks I'm a first-class nut."

"You are known for your eccentricities, Adam. The woman sounds astute. And did you litter her floor with sunflower seeds, as is your usual habit?"

Taking the handful of seed husks he was about to toss on the floor, Adam shoved them into his suit pocket and ignored the question. "Meredith Baxter is young and hopefully malleable. I don't want someone who's going to question my every decision. The most important thing is for me to gain permanent custody of Allison's children. I don't care if the whole world thinks I'm nuts. I'll do whatever it takes, spend however much money is necessary, to adopt Andrew and Megan. I promised Allison I would."

And Adam never went back on a promise. The attorney was living proof of that. At fourteen, Peter's parents had been killed in a car accident, leaving the young man virtually penniless. The Webbers' lavish lifestyle and opulent house on the hill had been a facade for a mountain of debt and unpaid bills.

Adam had convinced his father to take custody of Peter and see to his welfare and schooling. Allistair Morgan had never been a substitute father to Peter—he'd barely been a real one to Adam—but he had provided the monetary means for him to obtain a law degree. With the stipulation, of course, that upon passing the bar exam he would become the Morgans' family attorney.

The Morgans had a slew of business lawyers and financial advisors, but the shrewd old man wanted someone he could trust implicitly, someone who would look out for his children's interests after he was gone. That someone had been Peter, and it was a role he performed with dedication and devotion.

"I'm sure once Miss Baxter is apprised of the seriousness of your situation," Peter said finally, "she will view you in a different light."

Staring out the window, Adam watched the bustling traffic below. Thinking another light needed to be installed in the intersection, he made a mental note to suggest it at the next meeting of the Morgantown Planning Commission.

Frowning, he turned back to answer Peter's question. "The woman's a dreamer, a romantic. Besides, I don't care if she approves of what I'm doing or not. I'm paying her to plan and perform, not to ponder and pontificate."

The attorney's interest was piqued. Adam was usually nonplussed about most things. "Perhaps I'll stop by your house tomorrow morning and take a look at this wedding planner firsthand. She sounds intriguing."

"Meredith Baxter is not your type, Webb. She's a redhead, not a blonde."

"A redhead!" Peter's smile turned mischievous. "I've always been a sucker for redheads. They blush so charmingly, don't you think?"

Adam didn't know why, but for some reason Peter's comment grated on him. "I don't have time to discuss your taste in women. I've got more pressing problems at the moment."

Adam's mood had been foul and erratic of late, which worried Peter. The man hadn't had a date in six months; his sister's recent death had only complicated matters. Aside from business meetings and obligatory social engagements relating to the charities he funded, and that damned model train set he fiddled with, he didn't have much of a life.

"Maybe your problems and your attitude would improve if you went out with a woman. How long's it been since you've had sex? You live like a damn monk up there in that monastery you call a house. Engineer Adam must be running low on steam by now."

The gray eyes flashed annoyance. Adam hated being teased about his passion for model trains. His father had tormented him most of his adult life about his hobby. And he sure as heck didn't like being quizzed about his nonexistent sex life. "My sexual needs are not a topic of discussion, not even with you, Webb." Adam lowered himself onto a nearby chair. "So let's drop it. Maybe if you channeled your sexual desire into your work, you'd get more of it done."

"Is that what you're doing? Using your work and your business as a substitute? Because let me tell you, Adam, old buddy, that's not going to work. One of these days when you're least expecting it— *boom!* You're going to explode like a damn volcano."

Adam smiled condescendingly. "My, my, that is an interesting metaphor. It seems you and Miss Baxter have something in common. She likes to read torrid romance novels. I'm sure the eruption of a volcano has been used countless times to describe sexual climax in one or more of those lurid tales."

"Sounds to me like you're the one who should be reading them, Adam. You might learn something. And you might be able to experience love and romance vicariously through the pages of a book, since you're not performing it for real.''

''You're starting to sound like my mother, Peter, and that's the deadliest of mistakes.''

Peter was wise enough to know when he'd pushed too far, and from the dangerous expression on his best friend's face, that time had come. ''How is Lilah? Still exploring the mysteries of India?''

Adam's mother had left West Virginia shortly after her husband's death six years ago to travel the continent. She had not seen fit to return, not even for her only daughter's funeral, which was in keeping with Lilah Morgan's personality. She'd always loved herself more than anyone else.

Bitter at the slight she had shown his sister, Adam had also been relieved. He had no desire to see his mother, who would likely muck up the adoption proceedings with her histrionics, at any rate.

''Yes, thank God! She's still there. I just hope she stays away for the next three months, until we can get everything finalized.''

Peter hesitated before bringing up the next subject, which he knew would bring pain to his friend. But he also knew there was no getting around it. Adam wanted to be apprised of any and all developments concerning the murder of his sister. ''There's been no word on Curtis Tremayne. The district attorney's office doesn't have any new leads as to his whereabouts, and the private investigator we hired hasn't turned up anything yet. It's as if he's fallen off the face of the earth.''

At the mention of his former brother-in-law, Adam's eyes flashed quicksilver. He had warned Allison about marrying the handsome gold digger, but she'd fancied herself in love with Tremayne and hadn't listened.

Now she was dead.

The bastard had strangled the sweet, lovely woman with his bare hands after beating her viciously beforehand. The sight of Allison's battered body, when she was dying, had sickened Adam's stomach and his mind. He would never forget what his sister had endured for the sake of love.

The only good that had come out of Allison's relationship with Curtis Tremayne had been their daughter, Megan, and son, Andrew. Adam had promised Allison on her deathbed that he would keep the children from Tremayne and adopt them as his own.

"Hire more investigators. I want that guy found. It's been three months since my sister's murder, and we've had no justice, no closure. I want him to pay for what he's done."

Peter scribbled on his notepad. "I'll get right on it. Anything else?"

"I want the media contacted about my plans to marry. You can coordinate your efforts with Miss Baxter. You've probably had more experience in dealing with the press than she has. Though she looks a damn sight better than you."

The good-natured lawyer grinned. "You want national coverage—*Good Morning America,* the *Today Show?*"

Adam nodded. "I want the world to know that Adam Morgan is looking for a wife."

"You're going to make yourself a target for those who won't agree with what you're doing."

The tall man shrugged. "It's a small enough price

to pay to honor my sister's last request, don't you think? And I've got you and Miss Baxter to run interference for me." Adam finally smiled. "I think the woman is up for the challenge. How about you?"

Chapter Two

Meredith might have been bearding the lion at ten, but the only thing growling this morning as she made her way up the flagstone walk to the mansion's wide double doors was her stomach. She'd been running late and hadn't had time for breakfast.

Issuing a cease-and-desist order to her stomach, she sucked it in, tugged at the hem of her royal-blue wool suit jacket, checked her stockings to make sure they were run free—she wasn't going to give that voyeur another reason to stare at her legs—and quickly admired her manicure: Wild Rose, and not a chip in sight.

Let the cretin try to find fault with her today, she thought, smiling defiantly.

Banging the heavy brass door knocker three times, she turned to survey her surroundings while she waited.

The house sat atop a hill and overlooked the city below. The view was spectacular, she had to admit. The grounds were as well manicured as the man who owned them. The acre front lawn was as green as a piece of crushed velvet, unusual for this early in spring, and didn't have one unsightly weed growing in it. Not that weeds would dare grow in Adam Morgan's lawn.

Giving silent thanks that she didn't have to mow such a monstrosity, she smiled at the thought of her own postage-stamp-size yard, which suited her to perfection. She had more weeds than lawn, and what wasn't taken up with weeds was covered with flowers of every sort imaginable.

Flowers were her passion. She wondered if Adam Morgan had any passions, besides sunflower seeds, that is. It had taken her almost an hour to vacuum the carpet after he'd left yesterday. She knew now what Gretel had felt like following the breadcrumb trail.

Glancing at the plantings of white and red begonias lining the drive and front walk, she shook her head in dismay. Anyone with half a brain knew it wasn't wise to plant begonias until after Derby Day, which wasn't until May, and usually after the last frost. Not that such a thing mattered to Adam Morgan, who had more money than God, and probably wasn't the least bit bothered by such trivial matters. No doubt he had an army of gardeners who took care of such things.

Glancing at her watch to find that it was now five minutes after the hour, she frowned and banged the knocker again, harder this time, wondering why old houses never had doorbells. She was about to make an off-color comment about the rudeness of having been kept waiting, when the door was thrust open by the scowling man himself.

Adam Morgan didn't look at all happy to see her; the feeling, she could assure him, was mutual.

"You're late, Miss Baxter. I abhor lateness. It's a sign of a disorganized mind."

The attack was so sudden she didn't have time to ponder why his maid or butler hadn't answered the door. Drawing herself up to her five-foot, five-inch height, which barely met his chin, she responded, "For your information, Mr. Morgan, I was not late. I've been standing on your porch for a full five minutes waiting in the cold for someone to answer my knock.

"And while we're on the subject, I would think someone with your resources could afford an intercom system, or, at the very least, a working doorbell."

Tossing a handful of sunflower seed husks into the potting soil of one of the tall, spiral holly bushes flanking the massive front door, he stared at her as if she'd lost her mind. "A doorbell in a two-hundred-year-old historical house? I don't think so, Miss Baxter. Aside from the fact that it would look incongruous to have something so modern as a doorbell cluttering up the facade, it would ruin the exquisite stone—stone my great grandfather quarried himself and hauled up this hill on a wagon."

His voice was filled with such passion when he spoke about the mansion that Meredith's earlier question was now answered: apparently the house ranked right up there with sunflower seeds. Admirable.

"My housekeeper had an emergency and had to leave. If you're cold—" He stared at her chest, as if he could sense that her nipples were puckered, making Meredith extremely grateful she wore a suit jacket.

Not bothering to reply she followed him into the walnut-paneled study, where a fire burned cheerfully in the grate. The only cheerful thing about the room, she noted. The colors were somber and restrained, much like the man himself. The burgundy velvet drapes matched the two Queen Anne chairs flanking the fireplace. The leather-bound volumes lining the shelves, though attractive, and no doubt expensive, didn't add much in the way of relief. It was obvious the antique furnishings had been designed for looks not comfort.

Seating herself on a straight-backed chair fronting the impressive mahogany desk, she reached into her portfolio and pulled out an assortment of wedding invitation samples and cake photos, spreading them out on the leather desktop. "These are just samples, of course. I have others, if none meet your needs."

What would meet Adam's needs, or rather *who,* was seated directly in front of him. Meredith Baxter, with her bow-shaped, kissable mouth and a figure that conjured up X-rated thoughts, was an incredibly sexy woman. And as Peter had so succinctly pointed out, he hadn't been with a woman, sexy or otherwise, in a very long time.

"You're frowning, Mr. Morgan. Is there something the matter? As I said, I have other samples I can show you."

Pushing the material back to her, he shook his head. "Just use your own judgment, Miss Baxter. I don't really care what the cake and invitations look like. Those are trivial matters for the female mind."

Meredith bit the inside of her cheek, reminding herself of the ten thousand dollars sitting in her bank account.

"The only requirement I have is that the date be set for Saturday, June 21. I want the invitations printed immediately."

"But—" *Was the man insane? Duh!*

"No buts about it, Miss Baxter. I have a deadline to meet. We both do, as a matter of fact."

"But you don't have a bride. How can you possibly set a date for the wedding without a bride? Certain details have to be decided, and—"

"The wedding plans will proceed. I'm sure you're going to need every bit of the time allotted to pull this off. You have less than twelve weeks to finalize everything."

Realizing that she would probably be fired for what she was about to say, Meredith plunged ahead anyway. "Making wedding plans without a bride is the stupidest thing I've ever heard. I naturally assumed when you laid out your ridiculous scheme that you intended to find the bridal candidate first, then proceed with the arrangements. I can't plan a wedding without a bride. It just isn't—"

Ignoring her protest and pointed opinion, and without revealing so much as a flicker of the annoyance he felt, Adam moved from his desk to the floor adjacent to where Meredith sat and proceeded in his expensive designer suit to execute a series of sit-ups.

At the man's outlandish behavior, Meredith's mouth dropped open in disbelief. "Mr. Morgan!"

"I think better when I'm exercising," he said nonchalantly, as if everyone in America exercised in an Armani suit. "Care to join me? It gets the blood pumping to the brain." It also afforded one an excellent view of long, silky legs, which got the blood pumping elsewhere.

"In your case I don't think it's working, or else you wouldn't have made such a stupid suggestion."

Adam paused, then sat up, hugging his knees as he gazed into her earnest face—a face he was growing more attracted to with every passing moment. "I think you're forgetting who is paying for all this 'stupidity,' Miss Baxter. If I want to hold this wedding the day after tomorrow with a chimpanzee for a bride, I will.

"You've been hired to plan and execute, not to give opinions, unless they're asked for. I don't recall asking, do you?"

Meredith cursed inwardly as a flush crept over her cheeks, and she tried to keep her temper under control. The man was totally infuriating! He deserved to marry a chimpanzee. Preferably one who smelled bad and had large teeth.

Adam rose to his feet at the same time the study door opened and Peter Webber entered. The lawyer, who'd overheard the tail end of their conversation, smiled widely at the outspoken woman. Meredith Baxter didn't sound the least bit malleable. In fact, she sounded quite the match for the irascible millionaire.

"Don't let Adam intimidate you, Miss Baxter. He's very good at it, you know."

"Meredith Baxter meet my attorney, Peter Webber," Adam said, performing the introduction. "Or should I say *former* attorney? I'm thinking of making a change."

Peter smiled, not at all bothered by Adam's remark. The millionaire threatened to fire him at least once a week, sometimes twice. He had yet to carry out his threats.

"Nice to meet you. I understand we'll be working together on the media coverage."

He held out his hand, and Meredith took it, deciding in that instant that she liked Peter Webber. He was tall, very good-looking in an Ivy League sort of way, and he appeared to be a whole lot nicer than his client. The twinkle in his blue eyes said he didn't take Adam Morgan too seriously. But then, who in their right mind did?

"I'm looking forward to it, Mr. Webber."

"Call me Peter, or Webb. I've never been one to stand on ceremony."

"Me, neither. It's Meredith." Though she directed her comment to Peter, she was staring directly at Adam, who looked decidedly ill at ease, and not at all pleased that she and his attorney were hitting it off so well.

"You may call me Adam in private, Miss Baxter. But I'd like you to maintain the formalities in front of the press corp and when in the presence of my staff and business associates. At those times business protocols should be maintained."

"I'm all for keeping our relationship strictly business, Mr. Morgan, so you needn't worry I'll cross the barriers you've erected." She turned her back on the mogul, as if his concerns didn't matter at all.

"I believe you wanted to discuss the media coverage with me, Peter. I think we may have a problem with the chimpanzee angle." She met his grin with one of her own.

If anger could have produced steam, Adam would have blown it out through his ears. He was doing a darn good impersonation of Old Faithful about to erupt. Even the sight of the infuriating woman's too-tight skirt, hugging her impossibly firm, taut—

"Adam!" Peter called out for the second time. "Your phone's ringing. Do you want me to answer it?"

With a shake of his head, Adam cursed himself for allowing the wedding planner to interfere with his concentration, then picked up the receiver and was quickly absorbed in a multitude of work-related problems.

While Adam conducted business matters, Meredith and Peter discussed the various media strategies they wanted to implement. Peter suggested that they begin their campaign with local newspapers, radio and television stations, then work their way up to the national broadcasters, which made perfect sense to Meredith, who admittedly didn't know a press release from a grocery list.

They'd just finished their discussion when Adam's niece and nephew wandered into the room. In the space of a heartbeat, Meredith became enraptured.

The Tremayne children were adorable. To his credit, Adam had shielded them from the media circus surrounding his sister's murder, so this was the first time she'd had the opportunity to observe them.

At eight, Andrew appeared to be a typical boy. His uncombed hair looked like a bomb had recently exploded in it, the right knee of his pants was torn—Morgan was sure to disapprove of that—and his shoelaces were untied and trailing on the floor. The engaging grin he flashed made Meredith suspect the child would grow up to be a heartbreaker, just like his uncle was purported to be.

Two years younger, Megan was on the shy side

and hid behind her brother during Peter's introduction. Her two front teeth were missing, but that didn't detract from her dimpled smile when she chose to show it. A bedraggled teddy bear named Murphy was hugged tightly to her chest. The bear, Peter explained, had been a gift from her mother shortly before the woman's tragic death.

The attorney ruffled the boy's dark hair. "How's it going, sport?" Kneeling in front of Megan, he held out his arms. "Don't I get a kiss from my favorite girl?"

Meredith watched Peter quickly win over the little girl, who not only gave him a kiss but a hug as well. She noted with interest that no similar affection was bestowed upon her uncle, whose tone of voice had risen several octaves while he continued to berate one of his plant managers, making the child shrink further in response.

A few moments later Peter's beeper went off, calling him back to his office, and Meredith was left to fend for herself with the children, which didn't bother her in the least. She adored kids and hoped one day to have some of her own.

Engaging them in conversation, she soon had Megan and Andrew revealing all sorts of details about themselves, like how Megan hated brussels sprouts, how Andrew had broken his arm last year by falling out of a tree, and how their dog Barnaby was not allowed in the house because he tinkled on the carpet.

The children, laughing aloud at some of the silly jokes Meredith told, were completely at ease in her presence; the effortless, friendly exchange between them was not lost on Adam, who had a very difficult time communicating with his niece and nephew.

He was a man who talked to CEOs of major corporations, political figures and civic-minded leaders on a regular basis, but became tongue-tied and ill-at-ease when he had to converse with his dead sister's children.

Noting that Meredith had no such problem, Adam's previous pique was all but forgotten, replaced instead with intriguing thoughts and possibilities, and he heard himself saying, ''Why don't you stay for lunch, Miss Baxter, so we can continue our discussion of the wedding.''

Though startled by the invitation, Meredith's stomach, which had been rumbling like a cement mixer at the most inopportune moments, made up her mind for her, as did the two children, who were tugging her hands and begging her to stay.

''Please say you'll have lunch with us, Miss Baxter,'' Andrew implored, his sister bobbing her head in agreement. ''You don't have to worry about the food. Mrs. Fishburn made it before she left, not Uncle Adam.''

For once Adam didn't admonish his niece and nephew about butting into grown-up affairs that were none of their concern.

Meredith's heart went out to the two lost little souls. She couldn't imagine being so young and having to deal with the death of someone who comprised your whole world, and having to face the fact that your father, the man you were supposed to love and look up to, had been accused of killing your mother and was gone now, too.

"All right," she said, realizing her heart had suddenly jumped to her throat. "I'd love to."

OVER A DELICIOUS MEAL of chicken salad, fresh fruit and nut bread, Meredith and Adam discussed various locations where the wedding and reception could be held, finally deciding on the fashionable Morgantown Country Club, where Morgans had been members since its inception shortly after the Civil War.

When the discussion turned to bridal candidates, the children had their own advice to offer.

"Make sure the ladies you talk to like model trains, Miss Baxter," Andrew advised. "Uncle Adam loves playing with his trains."

Eyes widening, Meredith glanced up from her salad to observe the man seated across from her, wondering what else he liked playing with. Her knee started knocking and she grabbed it. "Is that so?" Adam's ears were as red as his necktie, and he seemed genuinely embarrassed, a fact she found quite charming.

"Yep. Uncle Adam doesn't let anyone—"

"That's quite enough, Andrew. I'm sure Miss Baxter isn't interested in my personal habits and hobbies." He looked to her for confirmation, but found none.

"Quite the contrary, Mr. Morgan. The more I know about you the easier it will be to find someone who's compatible, chimpanzees notwithstanding, of course." He replied to her teasing smile with an imperious arch of his brow.

"He doesn't like dogs, I know that," Megan said, turning to look out the dining room window at Barnaby, who bore a marked resemblance to Little Orphan Annie's dog Sandy, and was staring in at them with a forlorn expression. Barking several times, the mutt wagged his tail in hopeful reprieve.

Adam's voice softened. "Now, Megan, it isn't that I don't like dogs. But we have some very expensive Aubusson rugs on the hardwood floors, and the dog can't seem to distinguish between them and the grass."

"But Barnaby's lonely outside, Uncle Adam. He's just nervous because this is a new house, and he's scared of all the changes, that's all."

Meredith wondered if the little girl was speaking about the dog or herself. From the blank look on her uncle's face, it was doubtful he noted the difference.

"Rules are rules, Megan. And what did we learn about rules?"

"They're not to be questioned, but obeyed," the two kids recited in unison, making Meredith eager to jump across the table and shake some sense into the obtuse man.

But she wouldn't.

It was obvious Adam Morgan truly loved his niece and nephew, but was out of his element when it came to relating to them. Instead of talking to Andrew and Megan on a level they could understand, he spoke to them as if he were discussing a merger in a board-room.

It was none of her business. It was better not to get personally involved in the problems of a business client. Morgan would just have to work things out as best he could.

But the children...

She hated thinking that those adorable, lovable children would grow up to be carbon copies of their pompous millionaire uncle—hard, unyielding, unable to love.

Her appetite suddenly gone, Meredith made an excuse to leave and hurried out of the mansion, vowing not to get emotionally involved with anyone who lunched with three-fork place settings. And who didn't love dogs.

Chapter Three

Despite the bucolic name, Pleasant Acres Nursing Home was located downtown on High Street, only a short distance from Morgantown General Hospital on one of the town's main thoroughfares and within walking distance of Meredith's business, which is why she'd chosen the facility for her mother.

Louise Baxter's degenerative heart condition, which had been diagnosed as acute myocarditis two years before, was slowly killing her. Absolute bed rest and a proper diet were essential, and Meredith realized from the first that she would need help in providing the kind of adequate nursing care necessary to handle her mother's illness.

Stepping into the spacious black-and-white-tiled foyer of the brick building, which had been designed to look like Jefferson's Monticello, she waved to Flo Welch, the gray-haired receptionist seated at the entry station, and skirted around Henry Mullins's dachshund, who had escaped the confines of the old man's room again, with the hope, no doubt, of making it out the front door this time. Henry suffered from Alzheimer's, and he wasn't able to provide the dog with the kind of attention it craved.

Proceeding down the wide hallway, whose soft yellow walls always made her hungry for her mother's lemon meringue pie, she whistled at the colorful macaw perched outside Mrs. Hammond's suite, waved at the old lady seated in the doorway, then stepped next door to her mother's room.

Pets were an integral part of the nursing home's policy, and residents were encouraged to keep one. Meredith had yet to convince her mother that a puppy or kitten would be a good companion for her. Louise Baxter, though sick in body, still had a stubborn streak a mile wide running through her, and she'd never been overly fond of any of the many strays Meredith had adopted while growing up.

Entering the suite, she noted the middle-aged woman had one eye on the TV screen and the other on the clock resting on the nightstand beside her antique brass bed.

The nursing care facility did its best to make every patient's room as homey as possible from the red and gold chintz curtains at the window to the colorful braided rug covering the linoleum floor. In an attempt to make her feel more comfortable, many of the furnishings in the suite came from Louise's own home. Bric-a-brac and dozens of photos lined the windowsills and occasional tables, reminders of happier times in the Baxter family.

Meredith was a few minutes late and knew her mother was sure to comment, as Adam Morgan had commented this morning. She wasn't disappointed. "Thought you might be coming by, Merry, though I expected you a bit earlier. Is everything all right?"

She kissed her mother's cheek and worried at how pale she looked. The older woman's condition seemed to deteriorate with every passing day. Only a heart transplant could prevent the inevitable. But Louise's health insurance didn't cover it, and Meredith didn't have the resources to pay for the expensive operation and recovery period. The resulting guilt weighed heavily upon her slender shoulders.

Taking a seat on the love seat, she kicked off her high heels and wiggled her toes, emitting a sigh of relief, and wondered again for the hundredth time why she insisted on torturing herself for the sake of fashion. She should have followed the lead of that actress who wore tennis shoes with her business and evening attire.

"Fran Weaver and her daughter came in for a fitting of Heather's wedding gown," Meredith finally explained. "They got into a huge argument about the headpiece." She screwed up her face in disgust as she recalled the unpleasant incident. "I thought at one point they might actually come to blows. Heather was totally exasperated at her mother's insistence that she wear a rhinestone tiara instead of a traditional tulle veil." Fortunately, Meredith had managed to convince Fran that the tiara would not be appropriate with Heather's dotted-swiss gown. But only after Heather had burst into tears and locked herself in the dressing room.

"Frances always was one to put on airs," the older woman said, her tone clearly disapproving as she brushed graying wisps of hair from her ashen cheeks.

Frances Weaver had been one of Louise's cleaning customers after Henry Baxter's death had left his wife and daughter almost destitute. Though she'd worked hard to provide for Meredith, Louise had felt shame at having to clean the toilets of women who had once been her friends.

"What else happened today?" Her mother enjoyed listening to the day's events, eagerly awaiting even the smallest tidbit of gossip. Meredith tried to provide a steady stream of news to take Louise's mind off her illness and the loneliness that resulted from residing in the nursing home.

"Randall got an A on his criminal law test."

Louise's smile couldn't have been prouder had she been the law student's mother. "I know. He came by to visit earlier and brought me a half-dozen chocolate chip cookies. Wasn't that sweet? He's such a nice boy."

Meredith knew what to expect next, and she braced herself for it. Her mom made the same speech at least once a week. "I don't know why you don't think about dating him, Merry. A girl could do a lot worse."

Knowing Randall's dating preferences ran in a different direction from her own, Meredith smiled patiently at the suggestion. "We're just friends, Mom. I've told you that before."

"I want to see you married and settled before I die, honey. I don't want to go to my grave knowing you'll be left all alone."

"Now, Mom, you know I'm not going to let you die, so you needn't worry about that," Meredith said, wishing she really had that kind of divine power. At this point she'd settle for a magic wand—one she could wave and, with a flick of her wrist, cure her mother's heart ailment, find herself a Prince Charming and locate Adam Morgan a bride, so she could get the annoying man out of her hair.

"I'll get married in my own good time, and you'll be around to spoil the heck out of your grandchildren."

At her mother's sharp gasp, Meredith followed her gaze to the small television set suspended from a ceiling bracket in the far corner of the room. Adam was being interviewed on a segment of the local news about his plan to wed.

A handsomer man did not exist on the face of the planet, Meredith was sure of it, and she tried to ignore how the sound of his deep voice had the power to send tingles up and down her spine.

"What on earth is that odious man up to now?" Louise asked, not bothering to hide her dislike.

She fought the urge to groan. Her mother blamed the Morgans for her husband's death due to black lung disease, a condition he'd developed while working in the Morgan coal mines. Meredith had hoped to postpone the discussion of her newest client until she could figure out a way to break the news gently to her mother. Only now that wouldn't be possible.

"Isn't it a bit unorthodox to plan a wedding without a bride, Mr. Morgan?" Bill Simmons of WNPB News asked.

"A wedding? He's getting married?" Shaking her head in disbelief, Louise added, "Who would marry such a man? The poor woman must really be hard up."

"Uh, Mom, there's something we need to talk about—" But before Meredith could elaborate, Adam Morgan took the words right out of her mouth.

"I've hired Best Laid Plans to organize everything, from the bridal selection to the reception. Together we're planning a big event to mark my departure from bachelorhood to happily married man.''

Adam was smooth, she'd give him that. She only wished she had his facility with words, especially now, since her mother was staring at her as if she were Judas Iscariot in the flesh.

''How could you, Meredith? You know how I feel about the Morgans. They killed your father—they ruined our lives.''

Louise Baxter's face was unnaturally flushed, and Meredith knew that any kind of excitement or stress wasn't good for her. ''I was hoping to prepare you, Mom. I didn't know Morgan would be interviewed so quickly.'' She crossed to the bed, plumping the foam pillows behind the ailing woman's back. ''Now take a deep breath and calm down, or I'll ring for the nurse to give you a sedative.''

Despite the obstinate set to her chin, Louise did as instructed, much to Meredith's relief. ''I don't understand any of this, Merry.''

''It's just business, Mom. I needed the money that Morgan was willing to pay. I've got inventory to purchase, payroll to make, and Adam Morgan's offer was too good to refuse. After all, I *do* plan weddings for a living, and he *is* getting married.''

''Rich people always get what they want.''

''He doesn't seem like a bad guy. A little nutty perhaps, but not altogether bad. Morgan needs to marry quickly in order to gain custody of his niece and nephew.

''You remember how brutally his sister was murdered, leaving those two kids at the mercy of their deranged father?'' Louise tsked loudly, indicating she did. "Well, Adam Morgan is planning to adopt them and provide a stable home." How stable, Meredith couldn't be certain. After all, they'd be living with him. And he wasn't exactly what she would call sane by normal definitions.

"Allistair Morgan was scum. I'm sure his son is the same. Blood always tells."

Louise had more to say, but one of the nurses came in just then with her dinner, and Meredith was provided a reprieve, which she took without hesitation.

Kissing her mother goodbye, she said, "I'll see you tomorrow, Mom. I've got to get home and fix dinner for myself, let Harrison out before he pees on the floor." Harrison, her golden retriever, was named after Harrison Ford because he was so darn cute, and because Meredith had had a huge crush on the actor ever since Han Solo had piloted his way into her impressionable young heart.

"You be careful, Merry. And get all of your money in advance. Don't trust Adam Morgan."

Assuring her mother that she would only trust the man as far as she could spit, which wasn't all that far—she knew that, because she and her next door neighbor Ricky Trumble used to have spitting contests when they were kids— Meredith hurried out the door and headed for home.

PULLING INTO HER GRAVEL driveway ten minutes later, Meredith set the brake on the red Mitsubishi Eclipse and gathered up her things.

The amber light from the front porch lamp illuminated Peter Webber's handsome face. He was sitting on the brick steps blocking her door, holding a huge paper bag on his lap that smelled suspiciously like Chinese food the closer she approached. Her stomach, apparently forgetting the wonderful lunch she'd shared with the Morgans only hours before, roared appreciatively in response.

"Hi, Meredith. Hope you don't mind me darkening your doorstep without calling, but I neglected to get your business card before I left Adam's, and I didn't have your home phone number."

"If that's Chinese food, and if you've brought enough to share, then you're forgiven." Unlocking the door, she invited him in, and they were immediately assaulted by Harrison, who was as eager to greet them as he was to rush out the door to take care of pressing matters.

"Did you see Adam's interview?" He unloaded the small white cartons of delicious-smelling food onto the green-lacquered table in her kitchen. Like the rest of the house, the room was cozy, which was Meredith's euphemistic way of saying microscopic.

"It was a last-minute thing, so I went ahead without consulting you. Hope that was all right."

She waved away the objection and got down a couple of plates from the cupboard, fishing in the drawer for silverware and hoping to find forks that weren't horribly mismatched. Her housewares, like her furniture, were what Meredith referred to as eclectic, which sounded so much nicer than mishmash or garage-sale specials.

"I'm only involved in this media blitz because Adam wanted me to be. I'm not comfortable in the spotlight."

Peter seemed surprised. "As pretty as you are? I find that hard to believe."

The unexpected compliment took her off guard, and she smiled with a great deal of uncertainty. "Give me five minutes and you'll see just how hideous I really am."

Hurrying into her bedroom, Meredith tore off the uncomfortable suit and pantyhose and slipped on a pair of faded red sweats that had seen better days. Stuffing her aching feet into furry slippers that resembled white bunny rabbits whose whiskers moved when she did, she thought about removing her makeup, but decided against it. The poor man wasn't ready for such a shock before dinner.

Meredith emerged to find that the attorney had let the dog back inside and was now lying supine on the living room floor, trying to get the one-hundred-fifty-pound canine off his chest.

Harrison considered anything on the floor fair game, including, and most especially, people. "Harrison, leave Peter alone. It's time for dinner. Now go to your blanket. Shoo!"

The dog obeyed, but not before getting in one last swipe of his tongue down Peter's face. The attorney laughed, mopping up Harrison's exuberance with what used to be a clean white hankie. "Guess my idea of playing and your dog's are two different things. I've never been much good at wrestling. Is he always this friendly?"

She shook her head. "No, not always. He's very protective when the need arises, but he likes most people, especially when he finds one brave enough to crawl around on the floor with him."

Peter took a seat at the table situated near the window and began serving himself out of the cardboard containers. "Your attempt to make yourself ugly didn't work," he remarked, his grin teasing.

Meredith choked on her eggroll and reached for the glass of iced tea next to her plate. She liked Peter, hoped they would be friends, but that instant sexual attraction required for any good relationship was missing between them, unlike the spark that had ignited when Adam Morgan first stepped into her life.

Just her luck to be attracted to a nerdy businessman instead of a suave, handsome attorney.

"I bet you say that to all the ugly girls," she quipped. "Now pass the sesame chicken and tell me what evil media things you've conjured up for our prospective bridegroom."

WHILE MEREDITH AND PETER consumed gargantuan proportions of moo shoo pork, fried rice and steamed dumplings, the prospective bridegroom was having a difficult time concentrating on the paperwork in front of him.

As he mulled over P & Ls and production-cost analyses, Adam kept seeing Meredith's face, her incredibly long legs, her firm, lush breasts...

"Damn!" he cursed, his erotic musings having had the predictable effect. Moving restlessly to the window, he gazed out.

The moon was full, the stars shining brightly in a sky as black as his mood at the moment. Adam hated distractions, and Meredith Baxter was proving to be a very big distraction, if the pressure in his groin was any indication.

Perhaps if I call her... He glanced at his watch: seven-thirty. She'd be at home at this time of evening and would no doubt welcome a chance to discuss all those annoying, trivial wedding details that women were so fond of agonizing over.

What nonsense is this? Gazing longingly at the crystal decanter of brandy on the credenza behind his desk, he decided that liquor could eliminate the restlessness he was feeling far better than talking to an opinionated woman, who would no doubt ramble on about petits fours and champagne fountains and whatever else was found at wedding receptions. He hadn't a clue.

The brandy burned like liquid fire as it made its way down, but it didn't obliterate the memory of the smile on Meredith's face when she teased him about marrying a chimpanzee, or the genuine affection in her green eyes when she told those stupid jokes to his niece and nephew about embarrassed zebras and black-and-white newspapers. She'd left out the one about the nun rolling down the hill.

He smiled as he recalled Andrew and Megan's joyful laughter. The children hadn't had much to laugh about lately, what with their mother's death, and having to adjust to a new school and surroundings. But Meredith had managed to lighten their spirits, and had made them forget the ugliness of their situation, if only for a little while. Something he'd been unable to do.

He'd tried, of course. He truly loved Megan and Andrew. But he was out of his element when it came to children, schoolwork and the multitude of everyday problems kids seemed to have.

But he wouldn't admit his shortcomings to anyone, because if the courts knew how totally inept he was at being a parent, they would remove Megan and Andrew from his care, and no amount of money he could offer would make any difference at that point. If it hadn't been for Peter's persuasive argument with the court and the people at social services, Megan and Andrew would already be living in a foster home.

Over my dead body!

Deciding that his thoughts were becoming a little too maudlin, he put down the brandy and picked up the phone, dialing Meredith's home number before he could change his mind.

She answered on the third ring, and his heart gave a little *zing* when he heard her voice. There was laughter in the background—a man's laughter—and the sound of it knotted his gut.

"I'm sorry. I didn't know you had company."

"Mr. Morgan, is that you?" Meredith seemed genuinely surprised to hear from him. He felt like an ass.

"I'll call back tomorrow."

"No need. It's just Peter. He brought over Chinese and we've been going over the media campaign. We've come up with some wonderful ideas I think you're going to—"

"Peter Webber is at your house eating dinner?" he interrupted, and the vein in his temple started throbbing.

"Why, yes." He could hear the smile in her voice, which made him even madder. "Would you like to speak to him?"

Webb was the last person he wanted to talk to, especially now that he knew his so-called best friend hadn't wasted any time putting the moves on the wedding planner he'd hired. "No. I don't need to talk to Peter."

"Oh? Was there something else you needed?"

A gross misunderstatement, if ever he heard one.

"I was just calling to—" *What? Hear the sound of your voice? Talk you into going to bed with me?* "Get your reaction on the interview I did today. I thought it went well. Did you see it?"

"Yes. I was at the nursing home visiting my mother when it aired. I thought you did very well."

"I hear chimpanzees from all over the country are calling the station at this very moment trying to get a date with me." His attempt at humor was met with momentary silence, then she finally laughed, and Adam released the breath he didn't know he'd been holding.

She laughed! Adam's forehead broke out in a cold sweat. He'd never felt such relief, not even when Fergus Industries' bid to take over his corporation had failed last year.

"Did you make a joke, Mr. Morgan?" The teasing note in her voice was unmistakable. "I'm impressed. There's hope for you yet."

"I have my moments."

"Mmm."

The X-rated murmur went straight to Adam's lap, but was quickly dispelled when she giggled and said,"Harrison, stop that! You're tickling my ear."

Harrison? Who the hell was Harrison? Was the woman having a party? First Peter, now Harrison. How many men were at her house? He felt annoyed, left out, and wished he'd never called.

"Harrison gets off on licking my ears and feet," she explained. "He's such a pervert, but really very cute. He's also a bit too affectionate. I'm thinking of having him pruned. It may lessen his urges a bit, if you get my drift."

Adam's loins tightened, and he felt the strongest

urge to cross his legs. He developed an instant empathy for poor Harrison, whoever that poor, lovesick fool might be. "That's rather drastic, don't you think? Perhaps you should just tell him no. That's been known to work on occasion."

"Believe me, I've tried. But it just makes him all the more aggressive and amorous. He paws my chest, tries to rub against my leg. I—"

A strangled sound emitted from his throat. "Ah, there's my call waiting," he lied. "Gotta go."

Slamming down the phone, Adam took a deep breath, then poured himself a huge tumbler of bourbon and gulped it down, nearly choking in the process. He was as stiff as a two-week-old corpse.

The woman had no shame. She spoke of intimacies as if they were front-page news, as if she were working at one of those phone-sex hotlines, where all you needed was a preprogrammed phone dialer and a healthy imagination.

Unfortunately, Adam had both.

Chapter Four

"I quit!"

Meredith threw her purse down on the counter, knocking several bridal magazines onto the floor in the process, dropped her portfolio at her feet and dared Randall, who was staring wide-eyed at her, to object to her decision. Which, of course, he did.

"You can't quit, sweetie. You own the place." He came around from behind the counter and shoved a mug of coffee in her face. It was warm and steaming and smelled utterly delicious. "Here, drink this. It's mocha almond fudge and it's guaranteed to make even the most hideous problem dissolve straight away."

"Thanks." The chocolate aroma soothed her immediately. Why did anyone need tranquilizers when chocolate was so readily available? "I know I'm being childish," Meredith admitted, taking a sip and murmuring her approval. "But that—that man makes me nuts. He's so damn arrogant, so damn...rich."

She'd thought after last night that maybe he had some semblance of common decency and, well... normalcy about him. Granted their phone conversation had been strange and disjointed, and she'd never truly figured out why he'd called—the lame excuse he'd given about the interview just didn't wash—but she'd enjoyed their brief talk, even though he'd rudely slammed the phone in her ear. But every time she formed the opinion that maybe there was more to Adam Morgan than just a large bank account and an overabundance of arrogance, he went and did something stupid.

Guiding Meredith to the consultation area, usually reserved for prospective clients, Randall took a seat on the green-and-rose-flowered-chintz love seat and urged his distraught employer to do the same.

"At least he can pay the exorbitant bill we're going to charge him, right?" His grin was infectious, and Meredith finally smiled.

"I'm gonna stick it to him, Randall. You'd better believe it. I'm gonna nail that arrogant piece of pomposity for every grain of rice, every inch of ribbon, every damn candle that illuminates his glorious day."

"So, what'd he do? Make a pass? Try and molest you while you were strolling the sacred grounds of the Morgantown Country Club?"

Meredith pulled a face. "Hardly. I doubt Morgan has enough animal instinct to recognize that I'm of the opposite sex." Though she'd certainly recognized his gender right off, especially after a whiff of the heady musk aftershave he'd worn to their appointment. A fact that had made his rude comments seem all the worse.

With a disappointed sigh she explained, "We met in the grand ballroom of the country club, where the reception will most likely take place. It's a lovely room with huge crystal chandeliers, delicate French wallpaper and an oak parquet dance floor. Anyway, I wasn't there fifteen minutes when he looked me over from top to bottom in the most insulting way possible, mind you, and suggested in that superior way he has that I might want to wear something different to our next appointment.''

She looked down at her royal-blue suit. ''What's wrong with this? I know it's the same suit I wore last time we met, but my green one's at the cleaners, and I don't have the money right now to buy another.''

Randall patted her hand in a consoling fashion, his aggrieved expression clearly stating that Adam Morgan had overstepped his bounds and committed the cardinal sin: criticizing one's wearing apparel. ''What is he, the fashion police or something?''

''What he is, is a rich, snooty society snob who expects everyone to have had the same advantages as he. Well, I told Daddy Warbucks what he could do with his arrogant, rude and unwanted opinion. Then I did the only sensible thing I could think of.''

''*Uh-oh.*'' Shutting his eyes, Meredith's assistant braced for the worst, knowing the woman, as sweet as she was, had a wicked temper when pushed. ''Which was?''

''I dumped a pitcher of water onto his lap, told him to get over himself and stalked out.''

''*Sacrebleu!*'' Randall, who was taking French lessons, liked interjecting new words he'd learned into the conversation whenever he could. *Sacrebleu* and *mon dieu* were at the top of his list at the moment.

''*Sacrebleu,* is right! I think I just blew our ten

thousand dollar deposit and the future of this business.''

''I don't suppose you'd consider apologizing.''

Meredith jumped to her feet. ''Apologize? To him? Absolutely not! Are you crazy? The man is a Neanderthal. He has no social graces whatsoever, despite his privileged upbringing and fat bank account. I'm sorry I ever accepted the job in the first place.''

Meredith's adamant feelings were reinforced a few hours later while seated at the mahogany table with one of her most important clients, who'd come into the store to discuss possibilities for a mother-of-the-groom dress for her son's upcoming wedding.

The door flung open and a blast of cold air entered, along with Adam Morgan.

The wedding consultant gasped at the sight of the man, her face paling slightly, making Joan O'Connor turn her head to see what had caused such an overt reaction.

''I've come to apologize,'' he said, as if that would make up for his insufferable behavior.

He was wearing a different suit from the one Meredith had doused earlier—gray wool with a matching vest and pearl-gray shirt, which just happened to make the color of his eyes stand out—and he looked none the worse for wear. In fact, he looked mouth-wateringly good. Yummy, even.

Brushing the disturbing thought aside before she began to drool, she said, ''I'm with a client right now, Mr. Morgan. If you care to have a seat on the sofa, I'll be with you as soon as I can.'' She wasn't in any hurry to get rid of Mrs. O'Connor; the idea of making Morgan wait warmed her.

He stood beside the table, not moving a muscle,

as if he hadn't heard a word she'd said. "I'll buy you a new suit. In fact, I'll buy you a whole new wardrobe. It's the least I can do to make up for—"

It was Mrs. O'Connor's turn to gasp, though it was Meredith who turned beet red. The stupid man had made it sound as if she were his mistress, or kept woman, or whatever. It was obvious he'd given that impression to the stodgy matron, who was looking at her with shock and indignation.

Like Adam Morgan, Mrs. William O'Connor was one of the First Families of West Virginia. She'd even had the distinction FFWVA emblazoned on her personalized license plate for all the world to see. It was purported that her grandfather, Willy Fitzwilliam O'Connor, was the first resident of Morgantown to have owned and operated a thriving bordello, though Mrs. O'Connor adamantly denied the scandalous assertion, which had been made by a Morgan. The O'Connors and the Morgans hadn't gotten along since.

Forcing a smile, Meredith said, "If you'll excuse me one minute, Mrs. O'Connor, I need to deal with something."

The woman glared disapprovingly at Adam, then at Meredith, and gave a loud harrumph, clearly annoyed at the whole proceeding. "I'll come back another time. I don't like getting involved in matters that don't concern me. And I certainly don't like to be kept waiting.

"And you, young woman," she said to Meredith, "seem to have your hands full at the moment." With an imperious lift of her chins, and pointing her nose in the air, she turned and stalked out the door, leaving

Meredith speechless and standing with her mouth gaping open.

But only momentarily.

"Now see what you've done! You're not only ruining my life, you're ruining my business."

Adam stiffened, clearly not used to being castigated, especially by a woman—a woman he'd just apologized to. He did not normally apologize to anyone. "I can't be blamed for the rudeness of your clientele, Miss Baxter."

"Rudeness of my—" She threw back her head and laughed, but there was no humor in it. Rather, the sound resembled nails raking down a blackboard. "That's rich. You, of all people, calling someone else rude. How very novel." Actually, she knew for a fact that Mrs. O'Connor was extremely rude to most everyone she encountered and was prone to meddling in matters that didn't concern her, though she would declare otherwise.

"I said I was sorry. I offered to buy you a new wardrobe to make amends."

"I don't want a new wardrobe! I'm perfectly happy with the miserable one I've got."

Adam had never met a woman who didn't like or want new clothes. His sister had purchased a new wardrobe approximately every six weeks, saying fashionable clothing lifted her spirits. Perhaps the young woman was spirited enough. Or perhaps she was just stubborn and opinionated.

"My sister and mother always liked shopping for new clothes," he explained. "I thought you might, too."

She heaved a sigh, for it was suddenly quite obvious that the man was totally clueless and had no idea he'd offended her.

Where Adam Morgan came from money grew on trees, and the women in his life spent it freely, buying whatever they wanted with no thought to cost, designer label or starving children in India. Meredith, on the other hand, was on a fixed budget and spent only when it was absolutely necessary. Her business obligations came before her wardrobe, which admittedly lacked a certain flair and would probably have given Ann Taylor and Donna Karan heart seizures.

"Sometimes, Mr. Morgan, it might be a good idea to stop and think before opening your mouth. Not everyone has had your advantages in life. And it's not necessary to say every little thing that pops into your head." She wanted to say "your thick head" but she refrained.

He studied her. Meredith Baxter was quite different from any woman he'd ever known. She spoke her mind freely—albeit a bit too freely—was as organized in business as he was himself and didn't mind going out on a limb if her instincts called for it.

She'd so much as called him stupid over those wedding invitations. No one had ever dared do that before! But rather than be annoyed, he was impressed. He wondered if maybe he really *was* stupid.

"Upon further reflection, Miss Baxter, that blue suit is very becoming with your red hair and green eyes. And it certainly fits you well." Too well, as his body could amply testify. Only a surgical glove would have been more form fitting on her luscious body. "I shouldn't have remarked on the frequency of its use. I apologize."

"Apology accepted." She heaved another sigh, and his eyes followed her heaving bosom—up and down, making Meredith acutely aware that, though he was somewhat of a dolt, he was still all male. "Are we still on for tomorrow morning, then?" she asked. They had an appointment to review fabric samples. Adam Morgan intended to give input on the bridal gown and bridesmaid dresses, having apparently changed his mind about those seemingly trivial matters he'd spoken of previously.

"Only if you promise to leave your water canister at home." His lips twitched; her cheeks pinkened.

"Two jokes in two days. My, my. I'm blown away by your sense of humor, Mr. Morgan."

"Adam. Please call me Adam."

She arched a brow. "You're sure? Because—"

"I'm sure." He held out his hand, and Meredith took it. It was warm and firm, the knuckles lightly sprinkled with dark, masculine hairs. His hands exuded strength and confidence, maybe gentleness, and she was suddenly overcome with a pulsing sensation in her lower extremities that felt as if her heart had just gone into hyperdrive.

Good gracious! she thought. *I'm attracted to Daddy Warbucks.*

CURTIS TREMAYNE INHALED deeply of the cigarette clutched in his long, tapered fingers. His nails, once manicured religiously, were now jagged and dirty. He blew out a series of concentric smoke rings, then smiled sinisterly at the image projected on the TV screen—an image that provoked only one emotion: hatred for Adam Morgan.

"Rich bastard!" he muttered, stabbing the butt out

in a plastic ashtray that read Murray's Roadside Garage, and rolling himself off the lumpy excuse of a mattress.

The Howard Hotel wasn't exactly the kind of accommodation he'd been used to frequenting. When he'd been married to Allison they'd only traveled first class, dined in gourmet restaurants and stayed in five-star hotels. His wife's money had provided all the creature comforts a man in his position could want.

Curtis liked only the best, which was why he'd chosen Allison Morgan, the darling of Morgantown society, the spoiled, pampered pet of her ruthless father Allistair Morgan, who'd been as rich as Croesus and as mean as a junkyard dog. Curtis had hated him on sight.

Unfortunately, his wife was now dead, and he'd been cut off from all the Morgan wealth. Though he didn't mourn Allison—he'd never been in love with the foolish woman—he did mourn the loss of his Hugo Boss suits and sleek black Jaguar, which he'd been forced to leave behind when fleeing his former home.

It was a pity the way things had turned out. But, as usual, Allison had pushed his temper to the limit, always whining about his drinking, the women he fooled around with, the kids he never wanted and hadn't paid attention to.

Poor, love-starved Allison. She'd been such an easy mark for an experienced man like himself. A gigolo, they would have called him in the old days. He'd spent most of his adult life living off the largess of rich, lonely women.

Curtis hadn't meant to kill his wife, only to silence

her. But once he'd started slapping Allison around, he couldn't stop. Couldn't prevent himself from wrapping his hands around her slender throat. From squeezing it tightly to keep her quiet. From taking out his anger and frustration on a woman who'd never let him forget that he'd been born on the poor side of town and the wrong side of the blanket.

Big brother Adam had been her hero. Allison had never grown tired of singing the creep's praises, throwing his intelligence and business acumen in Curtis's face, until he'd wanted to puke. And it'd been Adam who'd convinced Allison to make Curtis sign a prenuptial agreement, preventing him from gaining control of her money. Even after Megan was born she wouldn't relent and discard it, or change her will to leave him as beneficiary.

A man could take only so much abuse.

Water under the bridge, he told himself with a shrug, lighting another cigarette. Damn things would probably kill him, if the police didn't find him first.

They were looking for him. He'd read the newspapers, seen the broadcasts and had reconciled himself to the fact that he would probably be profiled on *America's Most Wanted* soon. His fifteen minutes of fame wasn't quite what he'd expected.

Curtis was surprised he'd been able to elude the cops this long. What with Adam's vast resources and obvious hatred for him, he had expected to be caught by now. He'd been on the run for three months, practically living right under Morgan's nose, and they were no closer to finding him, if the police reports could be believed, than they'd been right after the murder.

But Curtis didn't intend to push his luck. Time was running out. He could feel it in his gut.

And so was his money.

The kids were his ticket to freedom, and as soon as he could figure out a plan, he intended to get them back and gain his revenge on Morgan in the process.

Chapter Five

Adam paced back and forth across the expensive Oriental carpet of the formal living room—a room designed to impress, with its exquisite brocade-covered antique furniture and gold-tasseled velvet drapes that Scarlett O'Hara would have been proud to wear. But it wasn't the richness of the furnishings, the Waterford crystal chandelier hanging from the hand-carved ceiling, or the Charles Wilson Peale portrait of Washington suspended over the marble-faced fireplace that impressed Meredith.

It was the man who was doing the pacing.

Meredith watched Adam eat up the space of the large room as he read over the latest schedule of upcoming media events, no doubt memorizing every detail.

For a man who performed a majority of his work behind a desk, Adam was well developed in all the right places. His thighs were quite muscular, and she was particularly impressed with his tush, which was compact, muscular, and…cute. Yes, cute!

Men probably didn't have an inkling that women noticed such things. But then, Adam hadn't bothered to hide his interest in her legs and breasts, so why shouldn't she look her fill of his cute little behind and broad chest? Turnabout was fair play, after all.

"These dates look fine to me, Meredith," he said finally, drawing her attention to his face, which was even more distracting than his derriere. It was totally unfair for a man to have such long, sooty eyelashes, such mesmerizing eyes, she thought with a sigh. "But instead of flying to New York for the *Today Show,* have Peter arrange for a remote broadcast. We can do the interview from the mansion."

The smile she flashed sent his pulse soaring, for about three seconds, until she said in a breathless voice, "Will Matt Lauer be doing the interview?" The very idea produced an enraptured expression, which annoyed the heck out of Adam, who seriously considered selling his shares in the National Broadcasting Company.

"Possibly. But he'll be in New York City, and you and I will be here." Thank God! He'd forgotten how shameless the woman could be. The handsome co-host wouldn't stand a chance, married or not.

"Matt's adorable. And he's got the cutest behind. Maybe not as nice as yours, but—" Realizing what she'd just said, Meredith clamped a hand over her mouth, her cheeks heating to infrared.

Glancing in the general vicinity of his "cute behind," Adam arched a brow and suppressed a smile. "Is that a fact?"

"Yes, well—" Meredith prayed for alien intervention. Now seemed a really good time for a space ship to zap her up and make her disappear.

Megan and Andrew bounded into the room at that moment, and she was so relieved and grateful she could have hugged them both. Their timing was impeccable. "Hi, guys!"

They returned her greeting, then walked straight up to their uncle, and Megan tugged on his hand. "We're bored, Uncle Adam," she informed him, displaying a great deal of womanly exasperation for a six-year-old child. "You said you were going to plan stuff for us to do today, and we've been waiting a long time, like forty hours or something." Her bottom lip jutted out, and she crossed her arms over her chest.

"Yeah. It's our last day of spring break, and we're wasting the whole day doing nothing."

"Don't be petulant, Andrew. I must finish with Miss Baxter first. Work always comes before pleasure."

"With you, work comes first all the time," the child remarked, rushing out of the room with his sister following close on his heels.

Adam seemed oblivious to the problem, and that worried Meredith. "I'm sorry," he said. "Now, where were we?"

Not anyplace she wanted to return. "We can continue our discussion another time. I think your niece and nephew need you more than I do right now."

"I've tried to explain to them about my work," he admitted, rubbing the back of his neck, as if the whole situation with the children was stressful and more than he could cope with.

"They're kids. You can't expect them to understand about deadlines and meetings. Work is boring to kids. They want fun, excitement. I was the same way when I was their age. And I hadn't just lost my parents."

Her perceptive comment hit home, and Adam heaved a sigh. "I guess I could take them somewhere, try to cheer them up."

She flashed him a smile, saying, "That's the spirit," then began to gather her things, which didn't sit well with Adam, who wanted her to stay. For some reason he couldn't quite fathom, the woman intrigued the heck out of him.

"There's a golf tournament at the club," he said, waiting for the horrified reaction he knew would be forthcoming. She didn't disappoint him.

"Golf? You want to take them to a golf tournament?" She rolled her eyes. "Boooorrrring. Why don't you just anesthetize them?"

He rubbed his chin, biting back a grin. "Hmm. I guess you're right. Maybe a tennis match would be better. It's a bit livelier and—"

"Good grief, Adam! You're hopeless. You can't take kids to an event like that. They'll be bored to tears in seconds. Surely you can think of something else. Something *fun*, perhaps." Did the man even know the meaning of the word? Not likely!

He shoved his hands into his pockets and shook his head. "'Fraid not. I'm not used to entertaining small children."

Her eyes suddenly sparkled with inspiration. "I've got it. What about a picnic? You could take them to the park. Let them go to the playground, run off some of that pent-up energy they've been accumulating all winter."

"Sounds intriguing." He rubbed his chin as if contemplating. "I might consider it, if you'll agree to go with us. I'm not sure I can handle them by myself."

Though the invitation flattered, it also alarmed Meredith. "What do you mean, you can't handle them? You're planning to adopt those kids. It'll be your full-time responsibility to care for Andrew and Megan after the adoption becomes legal."

He led her to the Chippendale sofa and sat down beside her. "I haven't told anyone this, Meredith, but the prospect of raising Megan and Andrew scares the heck out of me. I love them very much, and I want them with me—it's what Allison wanted, too—but I'm not sure I'm qualified to be a parent."

His confession moved her. For the first time since meeting Adam he seemed real, vulnerable...almost human. Taking his hand, she patted it. "You're going to be just fine. No one is born a parent. It's something that has to be learned. Once you find a wife, you'll settle into the role of husband and father in no time. I'm sure your instincts will prove as excellent in family matters as they do in business."

Her generosity warmed him. "Thank you. Now, say you'll come with us. It'll be far more enjoyable for the children if you do." And for me, he wanted to add.

She chewed her lower lip thoughtfully, and it was all Adam could do not to draw her into his arms and smother her with kisses. *A mouth that provocative should be outlawed!*

"I've got some jogging stuff in the trunk of my car. I guess I could change." She glanced at her watch. "My next appointment isn't until after four."

"Excellent. I'll go and tell Megan and Andrew while you fetch your things. Mrs. Fishburn will show you to one of the upstairs guest rooms where you can change."

"Are you going to change, too?"

He grinned, and two charming dimples creased his cheeks. Feeling suddenly oxygen deprived, Meredith sucked in some air.

"You didn't think I'd picnic in a suit, did you?"

Yes, actually, she did.

GARBED IN SHORT, WHITE jogging shorts, a shocking-pink elastic halter top that left little to the imagination, and sneakers, Meredith made her way back down the hall a few minutes later, hoping she could find her way downstairs without a tour guide.

The enormous house had a dozen or more rooms upstairs. The one she'd been given looked like something right out of the Palace of Versailles, with ornate gold Louis XIV furniture and a swimming-pool-size sunken marble tub that Marie Antoinette would have found quite to her liking. Meredith sure did, and would have loved soaking in it for the next hour or so.

The contrast of Adam's mansion to her little abode was sickeningly striking, but she didn't think she would change places with him. For all its glitter and glamour, the mansion was cold, austere and unfriendly, and looked more like a museum than a home.

Turning down another hall, she found herself at the entrance to another library, only this one had more than books in it, this one held Adam's model trains, complete with intricate scaled-down versions of towns, landscapes and miniature plastic people.

It was obvious a lot of time, effort and love had gone into creating the fantasy spread out before her, and she smiled softly at the notion that stern, autocratic Adam Morgan had a childlike side to him—a side he obviously didn't show to the outside world—a side that had been buried beneath years of breeding, tradition and proper behavior.

This new hidden facet of the millionaire intrigued her.

For years she'd harbored some of the same resentment her mother had held toward the Morgans. Her father'd toiled for the wealthy family and had even died because of it. She'd been denied finishing college, her mother had cleaned other people's houses, and all because they hadn't had the advantages of wealth, like the Morgans. She'd been weaned on resentment and had thrived on it.

But now Meredith could see that although she'd grown up poor she'd also grown up in a home filled with love, laughter and caring, while Adam had been raised in a mausoleum surrounded by servants and reared by parents who had obviously cared more about socializing at the country club than about nurturing two love-starved children.

Lilah and Alistair Morgan's warmth had been used up by charming their many society friends. There'd been little, if any, left over for their children.

Adam's inability to interact on a personal level with others, to enjoy the normal, everyday aspects of life around him, to relate to people as individuals pointed out that his upbringing had been sadly lacking in the areas that counted. Observing the Morgan life-style firsthand made Meredith better understand why he was the way he was.

She entered the living room a few minutes later to find that Adam had changed clothes, too. Though the navy linen slacks, white polo shirt and black-tasseled loafers were very nice and had probably cost a small fortune, they were still unsuitable for a picnic in the park.

"You're not planning to wear that, are you?"

He turned, about to respond, but the sight of Meredith's smooth, naked legs and revealing, next-to-nothing top, which delineated her ample bosom to delightful extremes, had him gasping for breath instead.

"Are you okay?" Alarmed, she rushed forward, breasts bouncing unrestrained, and Adam clutched his chest.

"Yes," he choked. "Yes, I'm fine. Just a little attack of—" *lust!* "—asthma." She pounded on his back.

"I thought you might have had something lodged in your throat. I know the Heimlich maneuver. I was going to wrap my arms about your chest and—"

And press those plump breasts into my back, thereby making my front protrude like a barber pole! He mopped his sweating forehead with a handkerchief. "I'm fine. Thanks, anyway. Must be the pollen this time of year."

Retreating a few steps, Meredith finally noticed Adam's overt reaction and swallowed her grin. Well, well, the man was just full of surprises. And he was just as impressive in front as in back.

"Megan and Andrew are waiting outside. Shall we go?"

"Uh, don't you want to put on something more comfortable, like jeans and a T-shirt? We're going picnicking not tailgating."

"I don't own any jeans, I'm afraid. My mother

never allowed us to wear them as children, and I guess I've never thought to purchase any.''

The admission should have shocked her, but it didn't. It just made her sad that he'd missed so much of the normalcy she'd always taken for granted. ''Well, Mr. Morgan, if I can spring for a new suit, you sure as heck can afford some jeans and T-shirts. They're staples in any parent's wardrobe. Trust me on this.''

And wouldn't his cute little tush look like dynamite in a pair of pre-washed Levi's!

BARNABY WAS almost as exuberant as the children, loping behind Megan and Andrew, barking and cavorting, trying to catch up to them as they scurried across the grass of Monongahela Park, situated on the banks of the river by the same name.

Laughing aloud at the dog's antics, Meredith said, ''That dog has a lot of personality. Megan seems quite fond of him.''

Adam didn't see anything the least bit redeeming about the mutt. ''He's a nuisance. I didn't want to bring him along, but the child—''

''Better watch it, Morgan. Your soft spot is showing.'' She flashed him a teasing grin and watched his cheeks redden.

''Just because I let you talk me into sitting on the cold ground when there are perfectly fine benches to use—'' he knew, because he'd donated the money to buy them ''—and just because I can't stand to hear my niece and nephew wail for hours on end about that damn dog, does not mean I'm soft.''

Reaching into the picnic basket, she brought forth a peace offering. ''Cookie?'' When he didn't respond, she shoved it into her mouth, making appreciative noises. "You don't know what you're missing. Mrs. Fishburn makes a darn good oatmeal raisin cookie, which just so happens to be my favorite cookie in the whole wide world.

"And we're not sitting on the ground. We're sitting on a blanket." Okay, it was a moth-eaten, oil-stained furniture blanket that she'd pulled from the trunk of her car, but it was still a blanket, even if it did smell.

Eyes fixed on Meredith's luscious mouth, Adam watched mesmerized as her delicate pink tongue flicked out to snag a crumb from her lower lip, and he decided he'd better do or say something quickly to get his mind off the woman's provocative mouth. "What I'm missing is work that's piling up on my desk as we speak. I don't know how I let you talk me into coming to a park when there's so much of it to do."

She stretched long legs out in front of him, watching with a great deal of satisfaction as his eyes followed the movement and glazed over. "Oh, don't be such a poop. And it was you who asked me to come, remember?"

A poop! No one had ever called him that before. Pulling his gaze up to meet her face again—a face that had begun haunting his dreams at night—he replied, "The kids respond better when you're around."

"Why are you so afraid of them? They're much smaller than you. And I doubt they bite."

"I'm not afraid. It's just—well, the way my sister and I were raised, I—" He shook his head. "Never mind." Trying to define his upbringing would have been next to impossible. Lilah and Allistair Morgan had a book of etiquette rules a foot thick about acceptable behavior that would have put Dr. Benjamin Spock's ideas of child rearing to shame. Adam called it the *Morgan Pedigree Encyclopedia.* "Make the grade or flunk life," his father'd been fond of saying.

"Why don't you play catch with Andrew? I bet he'd love to have his favorite uncle toss the softball around with him."

Adam's face lit, though there was a large measure of uncertainty mixed in as well. "Do you think so? I haven't had much practice. Even as a child I didn't play baseball very often." Actually, not at all...with his father, anyway. Every once in a while he'd been able to convince the gardener to play catch with him, but only when his parents weren't around.

"We were forced into golf, tennis, chess—activities my mother thought suitable and that would broaden our horizons."

How sad that a parent could stifle a child's natural ability and exuberance and not even realize it. Or care. "So here's your chance to show your mom that she was wrong. Baseball's America's sport, not chess, and I bet you've got a whole lot more motor skills than an eight-year-old boy. I doubt he'll notice if you don't catch every ball he tosses at you."

Looking unconvinced, Adam nevertheless pushed himself to his feet and took the suggestion she offered, calling out to his nephew, whose eager smile could have lit Wrigley Field.

A few moments later Megan plopped down on the blanket beside Meredith. She looked adorable in pink-flowered corduroy overalls and matching T-shirt. "You're sure pretty, Miss Baxter. I hope when I grow up I look just like you."

The child's comment touched Meredith, and she smiled softly. "Thanks, sweetie. But I think you're already much prettier than I am."

Megan frowned, shaking her head. "Uh-uh. My daddy said I was ugly. He called me a monkey, said I was a pain in the—" she pointed to her behind "—just like my mommy."

Drawing the child onto her lap, Meredith wished she had Curtis Tremayne in front of her at this very moment. The man really was a heartless fool to say such a terrible thing to his own child.

Adjusting the little girl's silver barrette, she inhaled deeply of baby shampoo and grass. "Don't believe a word of what your father told you, sweetie. You're a beautiful, smart and loving child. If I had a little girl, I'd want her to be just like you."

Her eyes widened. "Really?"

Meredith nodded. "Sometimes grown-ups have problems and take them out on their children, even if they don't mean to."

"Daddy hurt mommy. She went up to Heaven and won't be back to see me anymore." Her eyes filled with tears, and she buried her face in Meredith's neck, sobbing until the young woman's heart wanted to break.

Hugging the grieving child close, Meredith heaved a sigh. She could only imagine the horrors Megan and Andrew had lived through, were still experiencing, because of their mother's violent death. The children had been upstairs at the time of the attack and hadn't come upon her near-lifeless body until the following morning. It had been Andrew who'd called 911.

"I know, sweetheart, and I'm so very sorry. What your father did was terrible, and someday he'll be punished for it."

The little girl wiped her nose with the back of her sleeve. "Just like I'm punished when I do something bad?"

"Yes." Meredith decided it was time to change the subject. She didn't want to say anything bad about Tremayne, though she was tempted. But Curtis Tremayne, for all his ruthlessness and imperfections, was still Megan's father, and the child no doubt loved him, in spite of what he'd done. Children were loyal like that.

"Do you like to bake cookies?" she asked, and the little girl's eyes widened.

"I don't know. I've never baked cookies before."

"You haven't?" One of her fondest childhood memories was baking cookies with her mom. Louise Baxter had been a terrific cook. Meredith liked to think she had followed in her footsteps.

"Well, we'll just have to fix that, won't we? As soon as I have some free time, I'll ask your uncle if you can come over to my house and spend a Saturday. We'll bake cookies, watch videos and have a great time hanging out."

"Really, Miss Baxter?"

Meredith kissed the bridge of her small nose. "Really, Megan."

"Do you think Barnaby can come, too?"

Yanking playfully on the child's pigtail, she said, "Don't know 'bout that, squirt. We'll see." She wasn't sure Harrison would react very kindly to having another male dog in the house. He was very territorial, not to mention a big spoiled baby.

The child tore off like a shot to relate the good news to her brother and uncle. Adam turned after a moment and stared directly at Meredith. He had the most peculiar look on his face, as if he'd just found the cure for AIDS or had solved the world-hunger problem.

Meredith felt suddenly like Tweety Bird, who had mistakenly wandered into Sylvester the Cat's mouth, and she waved airily, trying to shrug off the uneasy feeling that assailed her.

But there was something about the eccentric millionaire's knowing, self-satisfied expression that sent shivers of apprehension tripping down her spine.

Chapter Six

Yanking on the navy-and-gold WVU football jacket he'd just purchased at the student union the previous day, Randall paused by the front door before leaving for the night. An ambulance on its way to the hospital raced by, sirens blaring, and he raised his voice to be heard above the din.

"I've got hours of study ahead of me, Meredith—there's a big test tomorrow—so I may be late coming in. Hope that's okay."

"I can handle the Prince of Darkness," she said with a confident smile, recalling Randall's new nickname for Adam. "Don't worry about a thing. Just ace that test. I'm expecting free legal advice when you graduate." With a wink she waved, watching him disappear into the darkness.

Moving to close up for the night, she was about to turn the dead bolt when Peter suddenly appeared through the etched glass of the door, accompanied by a blond woman she'd never seen before. Their unexpected presence startled her, and she clutched her chest, deciding in that moment, as her heart beat a wild bongo rhythm that would have impressed

Ricky Ricardo, that people could actually die of fright.

Yanking open the door, Meredith fully intended to give the attorney a piece of her mind for scaring her witless, but then his companion stepped into the light and she noticed the bruises on her face and discoloration around her right eye, and thought better of it. The poor thing had obviously been beaten, and not that long ago from the looks of it.

"Peter, I wasn't expecting you." She took several calming breaths, then smiled at the stranger standing next to him. "That doesn't mean to say you're not welcome." Ushering them inside, she took their coats and tossed them over the back of a chair, continuing a stream of mindless chatter.

"Meredith, I'd like you to meet Sally Jacobs," Peter said. There was an odd expression on his face as he made the introduction, the way his voice softened when he said her name, that Meredith found very intriguing.

The slender young woman with the soft brown eyes appeared to be about her own age. She glanced around the store, eyes darting to every corner, as if she expected the bogeyman to jump out at her at any moment, and Meredith suspected that the bogeyman had been a frequent visitor at Sally Jacobs's residence.

"Let me lock the door. That way we won't be disturbed by anyone," she said in an effort to reassure her, winning a grateful smile from the attorney.

"I'm sorry to be so skittish, Miss Baxter," Sally confessed, looking awkward and embarrassed at her paranoid behavior. "It's just that—"

"It's Meredith. And there's no need to apologize

or explain. I don't need a crystal ball to see you've been having a rough time lately.

"Come, sit down." She motioned them to the couch. "There's still some coffee left in the pot if you'd like some. Though I can't vouch for the flavor. My assistant's very fond of flavored coffees, especially anything with chocolate." Meredith considered Randall's penchant for sweets admirable but fattening.

"As you may have already guessed, Sally is a victim of abuse, at her ex-fiancé's hands." The mere mention of her former fiancé had the woman cringing, and Peter patted her hand in a comforting fashion, murmuring words of reassurance.

"I've been doing some professional counseling at the woman's shelter, offering legal advice, trying to help the women get back into the mainstream of society."

"Peter's been absolutely wonderful!" Sally's face lit up, suddenly transformed by her beaming smile, and Meredith thought she was quite pretty. Actually she thought Sally and Peter made a very attractive couple and wondered if the handsome bachelor thought so, too. Judging by the admiring glances he was casting in her direction, it appeared likely.

"We've just found Sally a small apartment not far from here, and I was wondering if you might be able to help her out with a part-time job. She used to work downtown at Beekman's Department Store before it closed, so she knows how to operate a cash register and work with customers."

Meredith's heart went out to the battered woman. Her hopeful expression held a large measure of desperation, and it was readily apparent that the woman's previous requests for employment had been turned down.

She didn't waste any time in making a decision. Helping those less fortunate than herself had been ingrained in her since childhood. Her parents hadn't had much in the way of monetary or material possessions, but what they'd had they'd shared with others.

"I can't pay much, minimum wage to start. I already have an assistant, but Randall's been taking extra time off because of school, so I can use someone to take up the slack. The job's yours, if you want it."

Tears of gratitude filled the woman's eyes, making Meredith doubly glad she'd made the offer. "I'll work very hard, Miss...Meredith. You won't be sorry you hired me."

"I'm sure you will, Sally. And I'm happy to have the extra help. It'll be fun having another woman around here for a change. Randall's a wonderful friend, but he's still a man." They exchanged a knowing look that spoke volumes, making Peter squirm restlessly in his seat. "When can you start?"

"Would tomorrow be too soon?" The excitement in the young woman's voice died suddenly, her eyes filling with uncertainty. "I'll understand if you want me to wait until the bruises fade." She moved a self-conscious hand to her cheek, and Meredith wanted to lash out at whoever had done this, wondering if the bruises inside the battered woman would ever disappear completely.

"Don't be silly," she reassured her. "I've got pancake makeup in the bathroom that could camouflage the Grand Canyon if we need it to. I use it when my face breaks out.'' Which was at least once a month. Zits at twenty-seven! The world was not a fair place.

The woman's laughter was rusty, as if she hadn't used those particular pipes in a while. ''Thank you. If it wasn't for kind people like you, Peter and the folks down at the shelter, I don't know what I'd have done. I was pretty much at the end of my rope.''

''Why don't you take a look around the store?'' Peter suggested. ''I'm sure Meredith won't mind, and I've got a few more details to work out with her.''

Sally's eyes sparkled with excited pleasure. ''Oh, can I? I just love anything associated with weddings.'' She cast a shy smile in Peter's direction that made his face flame.

Optimism in the face of adversity was something Meredith admired greatly; it seemed Sally was an example of that. ''Then you've definitely come to the right place,'' she said. ''The bridal gowns and veils are in the back room. Enjoy yourself.''

After she was out of earshot, Meredith turned to Peter. ''Thanks for bringing Sally here. She's going to be a big help. I like her, and I think we're going to work well together.''

''You're a kind woman, Meredith. I'm sorry I dumped this on you so suddenly, especially without calling. Guess I've been making a habit of that lately.'' He smiled ruefully. ''I was desperate. We'd already been turned down by eight different business owners in the last two days. Guess no one wanted to get involved because of the unsavory circumstances. You were my last hope.''

''That's what you get for thinking of me last.'' She heaved a sigh of mock exasperation. ''Men!''

"Guilty as charged. Speaking of which—how's it going with Adam? You two getting along okay?"

Actually, they were getting along better than she'd expected. Who would have guessed Daddy Warbucks could be charming when he put his mind to it? "Adam Morgan is an acquired taste, but I'm getting used to him."

"Adam's a good man. He just needs to find the right woman to make him come alive."

"And I'm doing my best to find that woman, counselor. We start the formal interviews next week. My message machine and post office box have been flooded with inquiries. In fact, Sally couldn't have come at a better time. I expect we'll get hundreds of phone calls after the *Today Show* airs next week. I can use her to field the candidates' calls, weed out the less desirable ones, that sort of thing."

Peter nodded, listening with half an ear to Meredith's plan to videotape the prospective brides, and all the while thinking that the perfect bride for Adam Morgan was standing right before him and she didn't even know it.

"WOULD YOU PLEASE look into the video camera that Miss Jacobs is holding and tell me why you want to marry a man you've never met before, Miss Fontaine?"

The big-busted, platinum blond, who'd obviously seen too many Jayne Mansfield movies—not that there were all that many—was, in Meredith's opinion, a cliché.

Popping her gum for the umpteenth time, until the wedding consultant wanted to scream, she checked her vampire-length, red-lacquered nails and replied, "I just flew in from Joisey."

"That would be New Jersey?" Meredith glanced covertly at Sally, who was rolling her eyes and trying not to smile.

"That's what I said—New Joisey. Anyway, I'm looking for a new man." *Pop, pop, pop.* "I dumped Wally back in Atlantic City after he told me that my thighs had jello-lotus, or something like that. So I says, 'Get the hell outta my life, Wally.' Anyway, I figured getting married to a millionaire wouldn't be that bad an idea." *Pop. Smack. Pop.* "You know, I'm getting kinda tired of taking my clothes off, and—"

"Just what line of work are you in, Miss Fontaine?" Glancing down at the questionnaire the woman had barely filled out, she kept her voice perfectly impassive. "Ah, I see…it says exotic dancer." Only it was spelled *X-otic.* "You performed at one of the casinos, I take it?"

The woman nodded, and her massive bosom heaved. Implants, Meredith decided with a certainty. "I saw that movie…you know, the one with Marilyn Monroe and Jane What's-her-name? So I figured, if those girls can find themselves a millionaire to marry, well then, so can I."

Blowing a bubble, which covered half her face, and which Meredith was very tempted to *pop, pop, pop,* Tess asked, "So, is this guy weird or what? Not that I mind all that much." *Pop, smack, pop.* "Wally was plenty perverted, believe you me, but—"

Yep. Adam was definitely weird, but not in the way Tess Fontaine meant. "I think that should do it,'' Meredith said, interrupting, not wanting to hear about the inventive Wally's lovemaking techniques.

Pasting on a smile, she wondered if they were ever going to find the meticulous millionaire a suitable bride. Obviously Tess Fontaine didn't fit the bill. Adam's words came to mind: *Intelligence being the most important quality, of course.* Had he said boobs, the woman would now be bouncing about the Morgan mansion.

''She's gone,'' Sally said a few minutes later, setting down the video camera, a huge grin splitting her face. ''I had no idea we'd be meeting so many interesting types of people. I just love this job! I feel as if I should be paying you for the education I'm getting, instead of the other way around.''

''Oh, you mean like Delissia Murdock and her boa constrictor?'' Meredith had nearly fainted when the attractive, soft-spoken Miss Murdock had primly opened up her large canvas carryall and released the slithering creature onto the mauve rug. Fergie, she'd explained, needed exercise.

Remembering the hideously large reptile still gave her goose bumps, and she rubbed her forearms against the chill. ''Wonder how Adam would like taking Fergie to bed with him? Talk about a heartfelt hug!''

Sally smiled, even though she'd been as frightened as her employer at the time, and had climbed up on one of the chairs, refusing to get down again until the snake was safely tucked away. ''I'm sure we'll get some better applicants next week. We were bound to get a few kooks in the beginning. I mean— this is a rather unorthodox idea and all.''

''Harebrained and idiotic, you mean?'' Meredith

didn't bother to hide her disgust. They had a little over nine weeks to find a suitable bride, and her optimism was at an all-time low.

The one bright spot in the whole miserable affair had been Sally, whose unfailing optimism and keen sense of humor made the situation bearable, if not almost fun.

Almost, because one would have to be a masochist to truly enjoy the predicament they presently found themselves in.

Sally's bruises had faded for the most part, and Meredith suspected that the young woman had laughed more in the past week and a half than she had in a very long while. Which almost—there was that word again—made pursuing Adam's ridiculous idea worthwhile.

Having just returned from the post office with more applications, Randall looked about the store, setting the three huge canvas bags he held on the floor, clearly disappointed to find no applicants remaining. "So, who'd I miss?"

"Remember that fifties movie star Jayne Mansfield?" Sally asked with a lift of her brows, and Randall's eyes widened.

"Really? *Mon dieu!* Now that I would like to have seen. I'll definitely watch the video. Should I bring popcorn?" He grinned, rubbing his hands together like a Wall Street broker expecting a windfall. "Who's next?"

It was clear he and Sally were enjoying the application process far more than their harried boss. "Hate to disappoint, but that's it for today," Meredith informed them. "I can't take anymore. My jaw's killing me from all the forced smiling I had to do."

''How many videos do you have to show Morgan this evening?''

A lump of dread filled her chest. ''You had to ask, didn't you, Randall?'' She sighed, not looking forward to facing Adam with such miserable results. ''Not counting the pregnant teenager from Michigan, who I convinced to return home, four. But that includes the snake lady and the Jayne Mansfield look-alike.''

''Mon dieu!''

''Exactly.''

''You forgot Thelma Packwood,'' Sally reminded her.

''Ah, yes. How does one describe Thelma, octogenarian turned manhunter?'' Tapping her chin, a mischievous twinkle lighting her eyes, she said, ''Come to think of it Thelma might be the one Adam's looking for.''

''She's a bit old for him, don't you think?''

''Now, Sally, we are an equal-opportunity bridal applicant agency. Just because Miss Packwood chooses to wear orthopedic shoes, elastic hose, has four-inch lenses, and is a firm believer in prunes, does not mean we can discount her.''

''Who knows? It could be love at first sight.'' Not that the old woman would be able to see Adam clearly.

Clutching her hands to her heart dramatically, she added, ''I can see the headlines now—True Love Blossoms for Morgantown Millionaire. Adam Morgan Woos and Weds World's Oldest Living Female. They'll probably make it into a movie of the week.''

Sally and Randall exchanged surprised looks, then

burst out laughing. Meredith couldn't resist joining them.

"I'm sure Louise will be very sad to hear that her daughter's developed a sadistic streak," Randall said. "What did the prince do this time to deserve your wrath, sweetie?"

Meredith frowned deeply, heaved a sigh and replied, "He hired me to find him a bride."

PETER CLUTCHED the gaily wrapped box, fairly certain that Adam, for all his business acumen, was too dense to get the meaning of what was inside.

After his last meeting with Meredith, Peter was more convinced than ever that she and Adam belonged together. She was wonderful with the children, had a terrific personality and sense of humor, not to mention a knockout body, and she matched the reclusive millionaire equally in stubbornness and intelligence, which, considering Adam's IQ, was nothing short of astonishing.

Meredith would make him the perfect bride. She had a lot of warmth and love to give, and Adam needed all he could get.

After his first meeting with the wedding planner, Peter had thought seriously about dating Meredith himself. He'd been thinking more and more lately about settling down, raising a family and buying a house with some acreage. She was the kind of girl a man thought about marrying—sweet, wholesome and just plain nice.

But after seeing her with Adam and, more important, after meeting Sally Jacobs, he knew fate had stepped in and tossed him a curve. Now if he could just do the same to Adam, they could dispense with this ridiculous bridal search idea and get on with their lives. Of course, convincing Adam of that would be next to impossible. Once he got a bit between his teeth, Adam ran like a Thoroughbred to the finish line.

"Hey, Webb. What brings you over?" Adam smiled at the attorney. "Mrs. Fishburn just told me you were here. Why didn't you call? You missed out on a great dinner of chicken *cordon bleu,* which I happen to know is one of your favorites." When they were kids, Peter had always managed to finagle an invitation for dinner on the nights the cook prepared the dish.

Hiding the small box behind his back, Peter smiled, wondering what Adam would think after opening his unorthodox gift. He didn't intend to stay and find out. Helping the man out with his love life was one thing, facing his wrath quite another.

"Meredith's due to stop over tonight with the latest bunch of videos, so I'm not going to stay long."

Guilt consumed the millionaire at the surge of relief he felt. As much as he liked his dearest friend, he'd been looking forward to spending the evening alone with Meredith.

"I just wanted to drop something off to you," Peter added.

"The Palmer contracts?" Adam furrowed his brow in confusion. "I thought you said—"

The lawyer shook his head. "No, they're not completed yet. Maybe tomorrow. Harriet's still working on them.

"I've… I've got a little present for you. I guess you could call it an early birthday present."

Now Adam really looked puzzled. "But my birthday's not for two more months, and we always go to Mama Francesca's to celebrate.'' Adam enjoyed good Italian food, even at small, unpretentious and inexpensive restaurants like Mama's. And he wasn't about to let Peter renege on a standing tradition.

Peter placed the box on the desk. ''Don't worry. Mama's is still on.'' He checked his watch, though he knew exactly what time it was. Adam's grandfather clock had just chimed seven. ''I've got to run. I'm helping Sally hang curtains tonight.''

A dark brow shot up, and a look of disbelief crossed Adam's face. ''You're hanging curtains? This Sally must be a very important client. I don't recall you ever—''

''Sally Jacobs is not a client, not in the way you mean, anyway. She's a woman I've been helping out. Someone I met at the women's shelter.''

''The one Allison helped found?'' The shelter had been one of his sister's pet projects. After her death it seemed more important than ever to continue supporting their work. Helping abused women escape brutality at the hands of their lovers, husbands or ex-husbands was a worthwhile investment, one he wished Allison had availed herself of sooner.

Peter nodded. ''The very same. I met her a few weeks back. She was bruised and battered and needed a friend, so I offered to be one.''

''But what do you know of this woman?'' Noting the way Peter suddenly stiffened, he added in a more conciliatory tone, ''By that I mean, maybe she's got deep psychological problems deriving from her abuse. As your friend, I don't want to see you get involved in something you might regret later.'' Peter had a habit of picking up strays and lost souls. He'd always been a soft touch for a hard-luck story.

"Always the careful one, eh, Adam?" Peter smiled, knowing his friend had only his best interests at heart, but also knowing that Adam was a careful man. Too careful, in many instances, allowing logic to rule his deeper emotions. And Peter blamed Allistair Morgan for that.

The austere millionaire had been cold and unemotional, probably a result of his own upbringing. Adam's father had seen everything in black-and-white, like columns on a ledger sheet. If it didn't add up and balance, it wasn't a wise investment. He'd seen people the same way.

Adam had never learned to think in shades of gray, to take chances that might not always be the safest course to follow.

"Sometimes you've got to go with your gut, old buddy. That's what I'm doing. I found Sally Jacobs a job with Meredith and—"

"Meredith hired this woman?"

His smile was decidedly smug. "Without batting an eyelash. And things are working out very well for both of them, I'm pleased to say. Sally's been doing the videotaping of the bridal applicants." And she'd become a different woman since she'd begun working for Meredith—more open, less tentative to give her opinions, eager to share her beautiful smile that never failed to take his breath away.

The dark-haired man took a moment to digest what he'd been told, then asked, "And you're interested in this woman?"

"By interested, if you mean romantically, the answer's yes. But I'm not pursuing that avenue right now. Sally needs a friend, not a lover. She needs to heal from the miserable ordeal her fiancé put her through.''

The vein in Adam's temple throbbed as memories of Allison's abuse and death flooded over him again. ''How badly did the bastard beat her?''

Every time Peter thought of how Sally had appeared that first time he'd gone to the shelter, he wanted to kill her ex-fiancé. She'd been so black and blue with bruises, it had taken weeks for her true complexion to emerge.

''Bad enough,'' he finally admitted, clenching and unclenching his fists, though he was unaware of the gesture, and trying to force his temper down. ''But she's almost fully recovered on the outside. I think it's going to take a while before she learns to trust again. They were only a month away from getting married. He cleaned out her bank account, stole most of her furniture and possessions, after beating the hell out of her first.''

Peter's anger was evident, and Adam surmised that his friend's heart was involved, which worried the heck out of him. He and Peter were as close as brothers—he'd always protected him, looked out for and taken care of him—and he didn't intend to stop now. ''Let me know if there's anything I can do to help.''

''Thanks. I'd better get going. Meredith'll be here any moment.'' As if on cue, the door knocker sounded. ''There she is now.'' Noting how flushed Adam's face had suddenly become, Peter was quite encouraged by the reaction. ''I always did have impeccable timing.''

Meredith wondered at the peculiar look Peter gave

her as he exited the house, then held up her bag of videos to Adam, who appeared somewhat distracted.

"Hope you've got plenty of popcorn," she said. "And maybe something strong to drink. I think you're going to need both."

Chapter Seven

Adam was not at home when Meredith stopped at the mansion to pick up Megan the following day. Mrs. Fishburn said he'd been invited to play in a benefit golf tournament at the country club and would stop by her house at the end of the day to retrieve his niece, if that met with her approval, which it did.

Meredith had been both relieved and disappointed that he wasn't home.

Relieved, because after last night's viewing of the videotapes, the man had been in the foulest mood. Even two snifters of brandy and Tess Fontaine's Jayne Mansfield impersonation hadn't put a smile on his face. Meredith, on the other hand, had been downright giddy, if not borderline hysterical.

Brandy and business definitely did not mix.

Adam just didn't understand why "normal, attractive and reasonably sane" women weren't jumping at the chance to wed him. After all, he'd explained with an affronted look, he was rich and not all together bad-looking.

Unable to dispute the obvious, Meredith decided it was pointless to lecture the man on the small, insignificant ingredient that was missing from his whole marriage scheme: love.

Sure, the money was nice. But who wanted to lie in a cold bed surrounded by a million one-dollar bills? That only happened in the movies, and only if you'd been fortunate enough to attract Robert Redford.

Not that Adam's bed would necessarily be cold, but—

Don't go there, Meredith.

And she was disappointed because she'd hoped to talk the stubborn man into accompanying his niece to her house for the day. Adam wasn't spending enough quality time with Andrew and Megan, and that worried Meredith, who'd grown inordinately fond of the children.

The kids needed all the love and emotional support they could get right now, and it was Adam's duty as their uncle and guardian to provide it. Andrew especially needed a man's guidance. Soon he'd be entering puberty, and then all hell was going to break loose.

Peter and Sally had graciously offered to keep the boy entertained for the day and evening, after Meredith had professed her guilt in not inviting him to accompany Megan. The couple planned to take him to a baseball game in Pittsburgh, and then afterward he'd be spending the night at Peter's.

Meredith was satisfied that Andrew wouldn't be missing out on anything, except perhaps baking chocolate chip cookies, but she intended to send two dozen home for him, anyway.

"How far away do you live, Miss Baxter?"

Without turning her eyes from the road, she answered the child sitting next to her. "Not far, sweetie. And you can call me Meredith. Miss Baxter makes me feel like a schoolteacher."

Megan giggled. "Okay."

"First we need to stop off and see my mom at the nursing home. She gets lonely if I don't visit her every day."

"Is your mommy sick?" There was genuine concern in her voice. "When's she gonna get all better?"

Braking for the red light at the intersection, Meredith eased in the clutch and threw the gear into first. Traffic downtown was heavy this morning. Many of Morgantown's long-time residents preferred shopping downtown to the mall off the freeway. She was one of them.

"I'm not sure she is, Megan. Her heart is weak, and she has to take things very slow and easy. She stays in her room most of the day." To finally admit to herself that her mother was likely to die in the nursing home had been difficult, but necessary for Meredith, who tended toward optimism and had forced herself to believe that miracles actually happened. This time, however, she knew that wasn't likely to be the case, no matter how hard she might pray. Louise Baxter was fresh out of miracles.

"Your mommy must get lonely. I know I do when Murphy's not with me." She gave the bear a squeeze. "Maybe we could get her a teddy bear, then she wouldn't be so lonely when you're not there."

A stuffed bear instead of a kitten or puppy. Meredith mulled over the child's brilliant idea, wishing she'd thought of it herself. "I think we'll stop at the toy store and do just that, sweetie. You can pick out a teddy bear to give her, okay?''

The child's face glowed at the prospect. ''Okay. We can have them wrap it all pretty with bows and flowered paper and stuff and say it's a present. Mommies like presents as much as kids do.''

''You're one smart cookie, squirt. I like your style.''

Leaning back against the seat, her little chest puffed up in pride, Megan turned on a pleased-as-punch smile and began to sing along with the radio.

A SHORT TIME LATER, bear in hand, they arrived at the nursing home. Louise had just finished eating her lunch and was staring out the window when they entered.

''Hi, Mom! I've brought you a special visitor.''

Turning at the sound of Meredith's voice, Louise's eyes widened with surprise and pleasure at the sight of the small child holding a large, gaily wrapped box. ''So I see.'' She shuffled forward slowly, her slippers flapping determinedly against the linoleum as she did, a questioning look on her face. The cautious child took a step back.

''This is Megan Tremayne, Mom. Megan's spending the day with me. We're going to make some of your famous chocolate chip cookies later.''

''Hello, Megan.'' Seating herself on the edge of the bed, Louise breathed in deeply, as if she'd just run a marathon, instead of crossing the small confines of her room. ''It's nice to meet you.''

''We brung you a present. Meredith said you was sick, so we thought we should bring something to cheer you up. Mommy always said that sick people needed cheering up.''

Louise and Meredith exchanged sad, knowing looks, then the older woman smiled softly and held out her hands. ''Your mommy was right, honey. Come sit up on the bed by me, so you can help me open my present.''

All traces of shyness gone, the child's eyes lit, the thought of opening presents too difficult to resist, as Louise knew it would be. ''Really!'' She didn't need a second invitation. ''Hope you like it. It's not as nice as mine, but it's pretty nice.''

They worked on the wrapping together, then the child lifted the lid, allowing Louise to tear back the white tissue paper. The sight of the teddy bear brought tears to the older woman's eyes. ''Why…why, it's wonderful! Thank you so much, Megan. I haven't had a stuffed bear since I was a child.''

Megan looked up at her cohort and grinned. ''See, I told ya she'd like it.''

''So you did, squirt.'' Meredith explained to her mother, ''Megan thought since she had Murphy to keep her company, you might like to have a bear to keep you company, too.'' Louise's gaze traveled over the brown, fuzzy bear, and then she hugged it to her chest. The longing in her eyes brought a lump to Meredith's throat. It was obvious her mother missed far more than good health.

''Bears are good for hugging,'' the child pronounced, and Louise leaned over and kissed her cheek.

''Thank you so much, honey. The bear's a very thoughtful gift. I'll treasure it always.''

"Whatcha gonna name it? Your bear gots to have a name."

"Well, I don't know." She looked at her daughter. "What do you think, Meredith?"

"You could call it Morgan after my uncle," Megan suggested, not waiting for her to answer, bouncing up and down at the idea, and not noticing how Louise had suddenly stiffened. "My bear's named Murphy. They could be twins—Murphy and Morgan."

Meredith helped her mother into bed, hoping she wouldn't say anything unkind about Megan's uncle. "I think we should let my mom call her bear whatever she wants, don't you, sweetie?"

Megan shrugged. "Okay. So wadda you wanna call it?"

Louise stared at the child's innocent face, then at the bear, who seemed to be looking back at her with an expectant expression. "I guess Morgan's as good a name as any," she conceded, making her daughter's eyes widen in surprise.

"Mom, really—"

Louise shook her head to forestall the objection. "I've always considered some of the Morgans to be over*bearing* and *bear*ly tolerable, so Morgan it will be." The corners of the woman's mouth twitched.

Glancing at the little girl to see if she'd been paying attention to her mother's caustic remarks, Meredith was relieved to find Megan thoroughly entranced by the television set and was suddenly grateful to the big purple dinosaur, who she normally could not abide.

Louise smiled affectionately at her daughter. "Thanks, Merry. I do love it. Warts and all."

"I'M GONNA BE POCAHONTAS when I grow up," Megan declared, stuffing another chocolate chip cookie into her mouth, then washing it down with a big drink of cold milk. "I think she's pretty, and smart, too." She wiped her mouth with the back of her arm, leaving a gooey chocolate stain on her sleeve that made Meredith wince. Mrs. Fishburn would not be pleased.

With two clicks of the remote, she shut off the VCR and television set and smiled, remembering how determined she'd been as a child to become Tinker Bell after watching the Disney production of *Peter Pan*. But no matter how hard she'd flapped her arms, the wings her mother had fashioned out of coat hangers and gold netting, and the sparkling glitter that had substituted for fairy dust, hadn't been enough to propel her into the air.

Children needed their dreams.

So did grown women.

"Let's make more popcorn," Megan suggested, and Meredith stifled a groan, clutching her stomach in response. They'd already consumed three large bowls. One more would likely land her in the ER with a stomach pump for a companion.

"I don't think so, squirt." They'd spent the last two hours watching the Disney movie and stuffing themselves with popcorn, cookies and pizza. Meredith was pretty darn certain that if she put one more morsel of anything into her mouth, she was going to puke. As it was, she'd probably gained five pounds for her piggish efforts.

"This sure has been fun. Can I come over again? Maybe we can watch *The Lion King* next time."

"Of course, sweetie. But next time I think we need

to pace ourselves better on all the junk food. I'm as stuffed as Murphy.''

The child yawned, rubbing her eyes. ''I'm sleepy. When's Uncle Adam coming to get me?''

Good question. Meredith had been wondering the same thing. Unfortunately, she had no answer to give Megan. According to what the housekeeper had said, Adam was to stop by after the golf tournament. It was now nine o'clock, and there'd been no sign of him, no phone call to say he'd be late. Of course, he was probably too busy hobnobbing with all his society friends to remember a small detail like his niece.

''He should be here soon, squirt. In the meantime, you can lie down on my bed and go to sleep.''

''But I ain't gots no pj's.''

''I've got something that can pass for a nightie. Follow me.'' She led her into the bedroom, handing the child a bright green T-shirt that read: So Many Books, So Little Time. Donita Lawrence, owner of Bell, Book and Candle, had gifted her with it, because Meredith was one of her best customers.

Well, it was easy to be a good book customer when you did more reading than dating, Meredith thought with a sigh.

Megan climbed onto the bed, and Harrison, who'd been dogging the little girl's heels all day, jumped up right next to her, unwilling to let his new best buddy out of his sight.

''I wish Barnaby could sleep with me, but Uncle Adam won't let him.'' She patted the dog's head affectionately, and the hound looked as if he was actually smiling, he was so in love with the child.

"But you've got Murphy to keep you company, sweetie."

"I know. But when my feets get cold, it'd be nice to have someone warm to snuggle with."

Meredith knew the feeling only too well. She'd been wearing socks to bed longer than she cared to think about.

RINGING THE DOORBELL, Adam glanced impatiently at his Rolex and frowned. He was late. He hated being late. And though he knew Meredith would probably be upset that he'd saddled her with Megan all these extra hours, it couldn't be helped.

Harry Whatley, the private investigator he'd hired to locate Curtis Tremayne, had shown up at the club just as he'd been about to leave. Unfortunately, the information the man had brought with him had been disappointing.

There were no new leads on the fugitive. The only encouraging news the investigator had offered was that *America's Most Wanted* had finally agreed to profile Tremayne in a couple of weeks. Adam hoped that broadcast would be the break they needed to locate his sister's murderer.

The door opened, and Adam pasted on a guilty smile. As he suspected, Meredith didn't look pleased. Her arms were folded across her chest, her foot tapping out a staccato rhythm. She didn't look pleased, but she sure looked adorable in her baggy blue-and-gold sweatshirt and tight leggings.

He brought forth a red heart-shaped box from behind his back. "Sorry I'm late. I had a very important appointment."

At the sight of the candy, Meredith almost turned

the color of split-pea soup. No one had given her candy in a very long time, so she tried not to be too unpleasant, though she knew the gesture was meant to salve the man's guilty conscience over being late. "Thanks. Hope you don't mind if I save it for later. I'm rather full at the moment."

He was about to say something else, but she didn't give him the opportunity. "I should be mad at you, anyway." But darn it was hard to be mad at a man who looked as good as Adam did in khakis and a navy-blue knit polo that delineated his well-formed pecs and biceps. The man probably had no idea whatsoever that he was a hunk.

Adam had the grace to look embarrassed as he entered the small house, which was attractively decorated, if sparsely furnished. "As I said before, I'm sorry. I guess I should have called."

"That would have been thoughtful." Something Adam was not. "You may as well come in and sit down. Megan's asleep, so there's no need for you to rush off, unless you want to, that is." She hoped he didn't. Meredith didn't stop to ask why, but Adam was growing on her like a fungus. She definitely had an itch that needed scratching.

Buy some fungicide, dummy. It's a lot less complicated than what you're contemplating.

He took a seat on the sofa that had once graced Louise and Henry Baxter's living room. It was orange-and-brown tweed—hideous really—and Meredith was suddenly self-conscious of her hand-me-down furnishings. "I've put most of my money into decorating the store, so—" She shrugged off the lame explanation.

Adam thought the house was quite homey, something his had never been, for all its opulence and cherished antiques. But then, it took more than furnishings to make a house a home: it took a loving family.

"I think your house reflects your personality."

"Simple, dull, tasteless?" she supplied with a grin, making him smile.

"I was going to say energetic, innovative and charming. I think it's warm and welcoming."

She looked about, but all she saw was old furniture, braided rugs with dog stains from when Harrison had been a pup and a television set that had probably witnessed the debut of Milton Berle. "Thanks. I've tried to liven it up a bit with throw pillows, candles and a few not-yet-dead plants." Outside, her flower garden flourished. Houseplants, however, were not her thing. Randall was always accusing her of committing planticide.

"Would you like a drink? Actually," she amended, "I have beer or wine. I'm not into the hard stuff. Most of my male acquaintances don't drink brandy." Most of her male acquaintances were pretty much nonexistent at the moment, but she wasn't about to admit that to him.

Randall and his friend, David, came over on occasion, usually when she was in the throes of PMS and feeling sorry for herself. Randall—bless him!—always brought chocolate.

No brandy! Lilah would have been horrified, Adam thought with a smile, liking the idea that Meredith was so different from his mother. "I'll have a beer."

"You probably want a glass, right?"

"If you've got one." He smiled as she hurried off

to her kitchen to fetch his drink. That she was nervous was obvious. The why of it, however, wasn't as clear.

While Meredith was occupied in the kitchen, Adam took time to ponder the strange birthday gift he'd received from Peter.

The gold-plated magnifying glass had taken him totally by surprise. He'd never been a stamp collector or a butterfly enthusiast, and Peter knew it. But odder still was the CD that had accompanied it, recorded by some singer he'd never heard of before.

It was a country music song. Adam hated country music, with all its twanging guitars and sappy lyrics about unrequited love. But he had to admit that the tune about looking for love in all the wrong places was kind of catchy. He'd found himself humming it on his way over tonight. But catchy or not, Adam still didn't understand why Peter had bought him such a bizarre gift.

"Damn!" Meredith cursed as the beer she poured too quickly headed up and spilled over the rim of the glass. Mopping up the mess with a paper towel, she hoped Adam wouldn't notice that he was drinking his brew out of a water goblet instead of a beer mug.

Sitting down next to him, she felt suddenly awkward and at a loss for words. Though she'd been to his home a dozen times or more for a dozen different reasons, it seemed different somehow having him on her own turf—on her lumpy sofa.

That he didn't belong there was obvious. The differences between them were glaring, like beer instead of brandy, popcorn instead of paté. Filet mignon to her hamburger.

Face it, Meredith, the man oozes class, while you merely sweat poverty.

"Is this beer from a microbrewery? I don't recognize the label, but I like it."

She nodded, relieved, betting that he didn't drink beer as a rule. He was probably used to Dom Perignon or Tattingers. She served both at wedding receptions, but she couldn't afford to imbibe the expensive bubbly herself. "I think so. Randall brought it over the last time he was here. You remember Randall, my assistant?"

He nodded absently. "I hope Megan wasn't any trouble. All she talked about all week was coming over here to spend the day with you." He'd envied the child that. He would much rather have spent the day in Meredith and Megan's company than knocking a small white ball into a tin cup. But Morgans had always hosted the benefit golf tournament at the club, and his attendance and participation had been expected.

With money comes responsibility. His father's daily lectures had pounded that edict and others into his brain. *You were born with a silver spoon in your mouth, boy. Don't choke on it. Morgans lead—they don't follow. No one respects a weakling. Be proud of your name, and don't ever dishonor it.*

Adam was relieved that his father hadn't been alive to witness Allison's death and the resulting scandal that had accompanied the horror. The old man would have been far more concerned about the Morgan name and reputation than about the great loss they'd all suffered. Adam suspected the adverse publicity was the reason Lilah hadn't come home for the funeral.

Tucking her legs beneath her, Meredith's eyes sparkled like dew-kissed shamrocks. "Megan's wonderful. I haven't had so much fun in years. She and Harrison got along famously."

About to take another sip of beer, Adam paused, mouth to rim. "Harrison was here tonight?"

"He still is. In my bedroom. Shall I—"

"Your bedroom!" The vein in his neck started throbbing. Meredith had a man in her bedroom, and she was entertaining another in her living room! Why was he so surprised? "Perhaps I'd better go." He made a move to leave, but she placed her hand on his arm, her eyes filling with confusion.

"Why would you want to leave? Although Harrison adores me, he really loves men. I know he'll be excited to meet you."

Adam fought the urge to bolt, but he didn't want to appear rude, and he certainly didn't want to appear jealous. Not that he had any reason to be. He and Meredith were merely business associates. She didn't mean anything to him. She was a means to an end, a pleasant diversion. If she had ten men in her bedroom, even twenty, he couldn't care less.

So why was his temple ready to burst? Why was his heart feeling twisted and torn?

Indigestion.

That was it. The food at the club had never been any good. He would recommend that the chef be fired immediately.

Rubbing his hand over his heart to lessen the discomfort, he replied, "That's nice."

Meredith whistled, then watched horrified when a moment later the huge dog came loping into the room, heading straight for Adam.

"Harrison, no!"

But it was too late.

The dog jumped up on the startled man, causing Adam to dump the remainder of his beer onto his lap.

"Harrison!" Without thinking, Meredith reached for a napkin and began patting up the beer. "I'm sorry. He's just overly friendly."

Harrison did his best to look contrite.

The touch of Meredith's hand on his crotch made Adam gasp, and he grasped her hand, trying to think of other things, but there was no way to prevent his very obvious reaction.

As Adam grew hard beneath her palm, Meredith pulled back as if burned, her cheeks flaming to the color of sun-ripened cherries. "I'm sorry. I didn't—"

"No harm done," he said quickly, taking a deep breath. "I didn't know Harrison was a dog. I thought he— Never mind." God, he sounded like an ass! He was an ass, he amended.

Forgetting all about being embarrassed, Meredith burst out laughing. "You thought Harrison was—" She grabbed her sides, laughing harder. "No wonder you sounded so pe…peculiar on the phone that time we spoke."

Her laughter was infectious, and he finally chuckled. "I'm relieved you're not in the habit of castrating all your male visitors. What was the expression you used? Pruning?"

"Stop! You're going to make me wet myself."

God, she was beautiful. Full of life. Warm and totally adorable. And Adam couldn't prevent himself from drawing her into his arms and kissing the smile right off her face.

Chapter Eight

"Mr. Morgan!"

"Miss Baxter?"

Eyes wide, lips swollen, tongue tingling, Meredith acted on pure impulse and wrapped her arms about Adam's neck, knocking him flat on his back and covering him with her body. He responded by thrusting his tongue into her mouth and deepening the kiss.

Anchoring her hands in his thick hair, she pressed her aching nipples into his chest, her groin into the hard shaft positioned between her thighs, and moved provocatively, trying to assuage the overwhelming need swamping her. Pleasure mingled with surprise; the touch of Adam's lips had sent her spiraling out of control.

Groaning like a man in the throes of torture, Adam moved his hands restlessly down her back, over her firm buttocks, losing himself in the sweetness of their kiss, in the sweetness that was Meredith.

"Watcha doing?"

Adam's hands, which were about to further explore the mysteries of Meredith's ripe breasts, froze, as did the rest of him.

Exchanging horrified glances, the couple broke

apart guiltily and righted themselves, before turning to face a very inquisitive six-year-old who was staring wide-eyed at them.

"How come you were lying on top of Uncle Adam, Meredith?"

Meredith's face felt as hot as every other part of her anatomy. Mercy, the man could kiss!

She swallowed hard. "Your uncle was just—" *What? Kissing me senseless? Turning my insides to mush?* "—helping me find one of my earrings, sweetie. That's all.

"Isn't that right, Adam?"

Wearing a pained expression, he nodded, crossing his legs and forcing a tight smile. His voice was rather high-pitched when he answered, "That's right. Meredith's earring." He made great pretense of searching the sofa cushions, coming up empty-handed. "It must be around here somewhere."

Meredith studied those hands that had so recently been touching her breasts and swallowed, thinking Megan had either very poor timing or had just saved her from making a huge mistake. She hadn't decided which.

"Don't bother. I'll look for it tomorrow."

Their eyes locked. Meredith's face grew warm again. Adam's mouth curved into a soft smile, then, scooping his niece up in his arms, he kissed her on the cheek.

"It's time we let Meredith get to bed, Megan." Wanting nothing more than to join her there, he let loose a frustrated sigh. "Why don't you gather up your things, so we can get going?" A blast of frigid air might be his only salvation.

The child held out her arms, and Meredith obliged

by hugging her tightly. "Thank you," she said. "I had a very nice time." Pressing her lips against Meredith's ear, she whispered, "I think Uncle Adam did, too. He doesn't usually smile like that."

Meredith bit back a grin. "I'm sure he did, sweetie. Now run, fetch your things."

By the time the child disappeared into the other room, Adam had reverted back to...well, Adam. He was in control. Reserved. All business. Meredith felt a twinge of disappointment. She rather liked the spontaneous, uninhibited version of the millionaire.

"I guess I'll see you on Monday," he said, stuffing his hands into his pockets—hands that wanted to caress, to explore, to finish what they'd started. "I assume you have more interviews to conduct?"

She tried to appear as unemotional and nonchalant as he, but considering that their tongues had recently been doing the mating mambo, it was difficult. "I do. Shall I come over in the evening as usual?"

He nodded. "Come for dinner. That way we'll have much more time to—" his pause was heavy with expectation "—look at the candidates' videos."

At the blatant desire she saw in his eyes—desire that mirrored her own, Meredith swallowed, not once but twice. "All right." Was that her voice that sounded so breathless?

After Adam and Megan had left, Meredith sprinted into the bathroom and turned on the shower to its coldest setting. She got in, clothes and all, allowing the frigid water to splash her full in the face, hoping it would shock some sense into her.

Kissing Adam had been totally irrational and unprofessional.

But wonderful!

It was by far the stupidest thing she'd ever done.

But definitely the most satisfying!

Would she live to regret it?

Probably.

"HOW DID YOUR DATE with Peter go Saturday night?" Meredith asked Sally. Unbuttoning her coat, she hung it on the hook behind the door in the back room, while waiting for her assistant to pour the morning's jolt of caffeine.

She needed something to keep her awake. She hadn't slept well these past two nights. Not since Adam had kissed her, made her aware that her body needed more than coffee and chocolate to sustain her. Her toes tingled just thinking about what had transpired between them.

A spoon clattered noisily to the floor, and Meredith glanced over at her red-faced companion, wondering what had made her so uncomfortable. The woman looked ready to cry.

"It wasn't a date," Sally protested. "Peter and I are just friends. I'm not ready for anything more." Though she'd been tempted to kiss Peter good-night when he'd walked her to the door. He'd wanted to kiss her. She'd seen the yearning in his eyes, felt and was flattered by the blatant interest he held for her, but she just couldn't take the next step.

Not yet.

Maybe not ever.

Dwayne had robbed her of much more than material possessions when he'd left. Her ex-fiancé had taken away her self-confidence, trust in men and desire for sexual entanglements. He'd left behind a woman who was hollow inside, whose heart and soul had been beaten out of her, who no longer trusted her own instincts when it came to members of the opposite sex.

"I didn't mean to pry. I'm sorry."

Sally smiled softly, handing her employer a steaming mug of French roast. "I don't mind, Meredith, truly I don't. It's just— I don't think I'll ever be able to be with a man in that way again."

Meredith felt compassion for her friend, knowing how hard it was to rebuild self-confidence once it was lost. She wasn't exactly oozing with the stuff herself. "Don't be silly," she said, wrapping an arm about her waist. "You've got too much heart to let that stupid ex-fiancé of yours get the better of you. I know in time you'll bounce back."

"But—"

Holding up her hand, Meredith was determined not to allow Sally to make excuses for herself. "I can only imagine the hell you've been through. But that's all behind you now. You've got to look forward, build a new life, find a new man."

The blonde didn't look convinced. "Trust me. They're not all they're cracked up to be."

"Your ex was just a loser. You haven't kissed enough frogs yet. Prince Charming may just wear a Brooks Brothers' suit." Or Armani, she added silently.

"I didn't kiss Peter. He wanted to kiss me, I could tell. But I just couldn't bring myself to—"

"If you don't feel that way about Peter, then you shouldn't feel obliged to kiss him. You don't owe him anything beyond gratitude."

Sally eased herself onto the cracked-vinyl-covered stool, and her deep sigh held a multitude of emotions.

"Peter doesn't expect anything. He's not like that. I wanted to kiss him. Deep in my heart I wanted to. But I just couldn't."

"You've got to give yourself time to heal, sweetie. I don't think our handsome lawyer is going anywhere anytime soon. I have the feeling he's as taken with you as you are with him."

Cheeks filled with color, Sally's expression grew hopeful. "Do you think so? I mean—he's so nice. I wish you could have seen him with Andrew. The man's a natural with kids." The memory brought a wistful smile to her lips.

"Unlike poor Adam," Meredith said, thinking out loud.

"So, how was your day with Megan? Did you two have a good time?"

Heat rose to Meredith's cheeks, despite her best efforts to conceal her embarrassment. "This coffee is really hot." She fanned her face, hoping Sally wouldn't notice, but the woman was too perceptive.

"Come on. Tell me what's going on. You've got that tongue-hanging-out-of-your-mouth look." Her eyes twinkled knowingly. "Did something happen between you and our staid millionaire?"

"He's not so staid."

Eyes widening, Sally grinned. "Really? Now this sounds interesting."

"Nothing happened. Well, not exactly nothing. We kissed."

"Standing or reclining?"

"Flatter than a pancake. We were on the sofa, and I nailed him with a flying tackle."

"You attacked the Prince of Darkness?"

"I prefer to think of him as Daddy Warbucks."

"Oh, wow!"

"Exactly. And you'd better keep this just between us, because if Randall gets wind, I'll never hear the end of it. He's not an Adam Morgan devotee. Except for his clothes. Randall does covet Adam's clothing."

"And you covet his body. Seems fair to me."

Blushing, Meredith replied, "What's not to like? For a man who sits behind a desk all day, and whose only form of entertainment seems to be model trains, he's in great shape." His lips were certainly in primo condition.

"Perhaps there's more to the handsome millionaire than just his money."

Meredith was certain Sally was right, and she intended to find out just how much more at dinner that evening.

STANDING SHIRTLESS at the gilt-framed bathroom mirror, Adam wiped the condensation from the glass with the heel of his hand before continuing shaving. Because of his heavy beard growth, he preferred a razor to an electric shaver. Filling his palm with a large dollop of white foamy cream, he lathered it onto his face and neck.

Andrew, who was seated on the rim of the tub, seemed fascinated by the whole shaving process, his eyes following Adam's every movement. "Where're you going tonight, Uncle Adam? How come you're shaving two times in one day? You don't always do that."

Scraping the blade down his jaw, he thought of Meredith's imminent arrival and nearly nicked himself. "Damn!"

In the mirror he saw the child's eyes widen, and he berated himself silently for using such harsh language in front of him. It was up to Adam to set an example for the children. He was all they had left now.

Andrew resembled his mother a great deal, and Adam's chest swelled with love, pride and sadness that the little boy would forever be deprived of Allison's gentle touch and sweet smile. She'd been a very good mother. A far better mother than Tremayne had been a father.

Adam knew what it was like to be ignored, to take second place to business meetings, social engagements and his mother's constant demands. His father hadn't had much time left to lavish on him when he was growing up, and he intended to try very hard not to make the same mistakes with Andrew and Megan. Tonight would be the exception, not the rule.

"I have a meeting tonight, Andrew," he finally explained, swallowing his bitterness. "Mrs. Fishburn's going to drop you and Megan off at Peter's tonight. You'll be staying the night, and he'll take you to school in the morning."

"Who's the meeting with? How come you're splashing that smelly stuff all over your face? My dad used to do that."

Adam paused, aftershave in hand, and faced the child. "Would you like to try some?"

The boy contemplated the offer, then wrinkled his nose and shook his head. "Nah. I mean—no, thanks. I don't wanna wear no smelly perfume stuff. That's for girls and sissies."

Hoping the child wasn't lumping him into either

category, Adam replied, "Someday you'll want girls to think you smell nice."

A mischievous grin split Andrew's face. "I bet Meredith's coming over here tonight. That's why you're putting on that smelly stuff."

Adam was amused at the young boy's perceptiveness. "Meredith's coming for dinner, then we're going to watch more of the bridal videos. It's a business meeting."

"Are you gonna kiss her again? Megan said you were mouth to mouth over at Meredith's house. That means you were kissing."

Heat rose up Adam's neck to land on his cheeks. "I could have been giving her mouth-to-mouth resuscitation for all you know. And you shouldn't be listening to the tales of a six-year-old."

"Then you weren't kissing her?"

"I didn't say that." A headache started to form, and he rubbed the back of his neck to ease the tension.

"Are you going to give her a baby?" Andrew asked, and Adam gasped, his mouth dropping open. "Davey Morris's mother is gonna have a baby, and Davey said his dad put the baby inside her. How'd he do that, Uncle Adam? How'd that baby get inside Mrs. Morris?"

In the bedroom Adam wondered if he should just lock himself in the closet until Andrew reached adulthood. Sighing at the absurd and cowardly thought, he dropped to the bed, unsure of what to say. "Uh. Well… I mean…"

The child flashed him a disappointed look. "Don't you know? Davey's dad knows. Maybe I should ask him."

Adam patted the space next to him. "Of course I know how babies are made, Andrew. I just didn't think we'd be having this talk so soon, that's all." Actually, he'd hoped that they would never have to have it. But then, did he want his nephew to learn about sex from his snickering classmates, the way Adam had?

His parents' idea of sex education had been to insist that Adam read the Bible, beginning with the Old Testament. And though he'd been titillated by some of it, all that begetting had confused him.

"On TV, the man and woman lie down on the bed, then the man gets on top of her and jumps around a bit, then the woman gets a baby in her. Is that right?"

The innocence on the child's face humbled him. "There's a bit more to it than that, son. You see, first two people need to love each other, then they get married, before they—"

"But those people on TV aren't always married, Uncle Adam. Sometimes they hardly know each other and zap," he snapped his fingers, "the man's jumping around."

Adam made a mental note to restrict Andrew and Megan's television viewing. "It's like this, Andrew—you don't necessarily have to be married, but you should be. When two people love each other they should get married before making any babies."

"But you're getting married, Uncle Adam. And you don't even know any of those women you might have to jump on top of. Except for Meredith. You know her. Why don't you marry Meredith, Uncle Adam? Then you can give her a baby." Andrew's face brightened at the idea.

What he wouldn't do for a drink right now, Adam thought, his temples pounding. "Grown-up relationships are rather complicated, son. Meredith and I are business associates. I like her, of course, but—"

Hmm. Marry Meredith.

"But you kissed her."

Heaving a sigh, Adam tried to explain. "Sometimes a man and a woman kiss, but—"

"Andrew, it's time to go."

Mrs. Fishburn's voice floated up the stairs at that moment, and a relieved Adam silently blessed the woman for her timing. "You'd better hurry, Andrew. You don't want to keep Mrs. Fishburn waiting. We'll continue our talk another time, okay?"

The child shrugged. "Okay. But if you decide to give Meredith a baby tonight, I want you to tell me about it. Promise."

In as controlled a voice as he could muster, Adam said, "I am not giving Meredith a baby. Now run along, or Mrs. Fishburn will leave without you." God forbid.

Unexpectedly, the small boy stood on tiptoe and kissed him on the cheek. "G'night, Uncle Adam. I'll see you tomorrow."

"Goodnight, son." Absently patting his cheek where the child's lips had so recently been, Adam heaved a deep sigh. Parenting was a lot tougher, a whole lot more complicated, than he'd originally thought.

He not only had to be a father to his sister's children, he had to be their teacher and guidance counselor, overseeing what they watched on TV, read in books, and who they associated with.

And he had to set an example for what was proper, moral behavior.

Good grief! The latter was going to be difficult, if not impossible.

Meredith would be arriving at any moment, and Adam wasn't sure he had enough willpower to resist kissing her again, to keep from exploring all the lovely hills and valleys of her body, to keep from lying on top of her and doing a little "jumping around."

Chapter Nine

Staring wide-eyed at the image on the television screen, Adam didn't bother to hide his disgust. The woman had yellow—not blond but yellow—short, spiked hair, wore camouflage pants, combat boots and looked as if she could press at least 350 pounds with one hand tied behind her back.

He'd always considered himself to be in good physical condition—he swam almost every day—but the woman in the video made him feel like a 190-pound weakling.

"Are these women for real?" he asked. "Or are you just making them up?" Adam suspected Meredith was only showing him the very worst candidates. Surely there had to be one normal woman left in the world he could marry.

Meredith smiled innocently. "I assure you Miss Wallace—Randall calls her G.I. Jane—is a perfectly legitimate candidate. She responded after your last television interview, said she could whip you into shape in no time. Not that you aren't in good shape," she added quickly when his brows rose to his hairline. "You seem very well developed to me."

"So do you." His eyes caressed her with agonizing thoroughness, and Meredith felt her face heat and her nipples harden. She wished now she hadn't worn the revealing backless sundress. It was hardly appropriate attire for a business meeting, or a Morgantown spring evening—it was actually quite chilly outside. But the slinky black dress had always made her feel sexy, and she needed to boost her self-confidence, which had been flagging lately.

Interviewing all those gorgeous, intelligent women had taken its toll. She felt dowdy as a brown wren and dumb as a box of rocks compared to most of them. Some had Ph.D.s; she had good intentions.

Adam would never view most of the videos she'd filmed and never meet the candidates. Just because the women were pretty and smart didn't mean they were right for the millionaire. It was her responsibility—her duty—to weed them out, and Meredith took that responsibility very seriously. It might take a few more business meetings to find just the right person.

As much as they both pretended that tonight was a typical business meeting, Meredith knew it was anything but. The staff had been given the night off, the kids were staying overnight at Peter's house, and she had yet to be served dinner, although it was nearly half past eight.

The game they were playing was dangerous. If she wasn't careful, she could come out the loser. Thus far, her dating scorecard had been rather abysmal. None of the men had fit her Prince Charming qualifications.

Until now.

Adam fit them about as well as the Levi's hugging his powerful thighs. She was pleased he'd taken her advice and purchased them. Though she hadn't expected him to look so darned appealing.

Everything about the man was appealing. She adored the musky scent of his cologne, the way his forearm muscles corded whenever he lifted something heavy, the mesmerizing silver of his eyes when he gazed intently at her, making her toes curl heavenward.

Turning off the video player, Adam clicked on the stereo and scooted closer to Meredith. "You look lovely tonight. I like your dress." Lifting the thin shoulder strap, his hand inching dangerously close to her breast, he leaned forward and inhaled deeply. "And you smell positively intoxicating."

"Th-thank you." She swallowed, wondering what she would do if his hand continued to venture downward. Not trusting herself enough to find out, she said, "Uh…I hate to be rude, but didn't you mention something about dinner? I'm starving. I—"

Cupping the back of her neck, he drew her toward him. "We'll eat later. I promise."

What he was promising was reflected in his eyes, and it made gooseflesh erupt over her arms. "Later?" she croaked before his lips descended and all thought processes shut down.

He traced the soft fullness of her lower lip with his tongue before plunging inside to send shivers of desire rushing through her. It was a heart-pounding, blood-racing, whopper of a kiss. On a scale of one to ten, it rated fifteen! Her socks would have been knocked off had she been wearing any.

Lifting his head, Adam gazed into eyes filled with passion. "I've been thinking about doing that since we got interrupted Saturday night. I like kissing you.''

She licked her lips self-consciously. ''I like kissing you, too. But I—''

''I want you.''

Well, that was certainly honest enough. Not knowing quite how to respond to such a blatant declaration, Meredith sought safety by changing the subject. ''Megan tells me you have an indoor pool.'' She eased out of his embrace, putting distance between them. ''Do you use it much?''

Disappointment took a backseat to a newly hatched plan. ''Every day. Would you like to see it? Perhaps we can take a swim. Cool things off a bit.''

Cooling things off seemed a very good idea. Bone meltdown was likely to occur if he kissed her again. ''I'd like that.'' It would give them time to think, time to realize that what they were contemplating was totally irrational, if not downright stupid.

A few minutes later they entered the pool house, which was located on the ground floor. The Olympic-size pool was partly indoors and partly out. A spa bubbled enticingly at the far end of the inside portion, like a potent witch's brew promising untold delights. Dressing rooms occupied one side of the enclosure, and a small kitchen, complete with soda fountain, encompassed the other.

Meredith began to perspire. Actually she was sweating. But her mother always said that ladies didn't sweat, they glistened like dewdrops on newly formed leaves. Dewdrops or not, she was dripping like a leaky faucet, and she wasn't altogether certain that the humid condition inside the pool area had anything to do with it.

She felt nervous, excited and very apprehensive. She'd been the same way once before: the night she'd given her virginity to Jason Davis in the backseat of his 85 Mercury Cougar. Jason had been a huge mistake. Would Adam be one, too?

"I don't have a bathing suit."

"We have two choices then—we can both swim in the nude, which I prefer, or you can use one of the suits that are kept in the dressing rooms for the guests."

How many "guests" had come before her? she wondered. And why wasn't he marrying one of them? "I think I'll wear one of the suits."

"I suppose you'd like me to wear one, too?"

She nodded, trying hard not to look so relieved. She wasn't a prude, but she wasn't Lady Godiva, either. Who would've guessed Adam Morgan would be a candidate for a nudist colony? "Yes, please." For a supposedly staid businessman, the man had some rather outlandish ideas. But then, she already knew he was different. He was advertising for a wife, after all.

With the sexiest grin, which displayed a dimple in his left cheek, he showed her where to change and entered the dressing room to the left of hers.

When had Daddy Warbucks turned into Mel Gibson?

It didn't take Meredith long to slip out of her dress. But what she found to replace it left her staring openmouthed at her reflection in the mirror.

The black string bikini—the only suit that came close to fitting—was nothing short of indecent, leaving Meredith to conclude that all of the women who'd come before her had been anorexic.

To a woman used to wearing a modest one-piece swimsuit, the brief bikini was shocking. Her breasts overflowed the cups—what little there was of them—and the tiny piece of black triangle that was supposed to cover her lower area was next to nonexistent. To say she felt exposed was an understatement!

Well, she'd wanted to feel sexy tonight, and this little number certainly did the trick.

Thank heavens she had shaved her legs this morning!

"What's taking so long? Do you need help?"

Was that hope or urgency she heard in Adam's voice? Suddenly she felt like an insect who'd been lured into the spider's web. "I'll be out in a minute." *Just as soon as my skin color fades to normal.*

He was in the pool when she exited the dressing room, and the look he flashed her could have heated the spa and ignited wet firewood all on its own.

"Judas Priest!" His mouth fell open.

"Exactly." Though she was secretly glad he liked what he saw. It was a definite boost to her ego.

Submerged in the eighty-degree water, Adam's member lengthened to the size of a barber pole. His heated gaze was fixed on Meredith's bouncing breasts as she strolled self-consciously toward the pool, looking like some mythical water nymph. "I see you found something that fit."

Without commenting on the debatable observation, she dove in, surfacing right beside him, white flesh glistening, tempting and too inviting to resist. He reached for her, but she laughed, slapping playfully at his hands before swimming away.

"We're supposed to be cooling off, remember?"

He caught up with her quickly, grasping her foot

as she tried to escape and pulling her toward him. "Not so fast, mermaid." Wrapping his arms around her waist, he pressed those glorious breasts into his chest and captured her lips.

Resistance is futile, Meredith thought. Hadn't the Borg said that on Star Trek? The phrase fit her situation to a tee.

Like English ivy, she draped her arms around his neck and gave as good as she got, plunging her tongue into his hot mouth and tasting the manliness that was Adam.

Chocolates paled in comparison.

By the time she opened her eyes her suit top was gone and Adam's strong hands had replaced it. With tantalizing slowness he fondled her breasts, teased her nipples into erect peaks, then lifted her onto the step, replacing his hands with his mouth and tongue.

Meredith felt as if she was drowning, and she wasn't even in the water!

The urge to abandon all common sense was overwhelming. She fought it, tried to ignore the way her bones were melting, her nipples rock hard and tingling, but when he lifted the lower edge of her suit and began to explore her femininity, she was lost.

Needing Adam inside her, she boldly reached out to cup his maleness and stroke the long length of him, tugging down his trunks to reveal every glorious inch of his body. Her suit soon followed his to float atop the water like sacrificial offerings to the love god Eros.

"We should probably go upstairs to my bed, but I can't wait," he admitted, his brow and upper lip beaded with sweat, his eyes glittering with desire.

Wait! Was he kidding? She was ready to give water aerobics a whole new meaning. "Me, neither." Taking the initiative, she wrapped her legs around his waist, held on to his broad shoulders with her hands and impaled herself.

Clasping her buttocks, he plunged in the rest of the way, thrusting into her with strong, swift strokes, taking her nipple between his lips and caressing it with his tongue, devouring her breasts like a starving man who had an insatiable appetite.

The tension building, she met him stroke for stroke, the buoyancy of the water lifting her, higher, ever higher. At last with one deep thrust, he took her over the top, and they climaxed together.

After their breathing had become somewhat normal, Adam continued to hug her gently, kissing her ear, her neck, whispering how beautiful she was, how absolutely wonderful, which was exactly how Meredith felt at the moment.

Perfect. Wonderful. Romantic. All those adjectives came to mind to describe her union with Adam.

"Are you all right?" he asked, concerned that she hadn't said a word. He didn't want her to regret what had happened. Something that felt so right, so good, shouldn't be cause for regret. He certainly had none. Making love with Meredith had been one of, if not *the* most satisfying experiences of his life.

"Of course, I'm not all right. I've just been thoroughly ravished, as they say in those romance novels you so disdain, and I adored every minute of it." Her grin was decidedly naughty.

"I've never met anyone like you before."

A look of mock indignation crossed her face. "I should hope not! I'm a unique individual."

"Shall we continue this upstairs? I'm starting to shrivel in the most unfortunate places."

Her hand slid down the length of him, and he met the challenge admirably. "Yes. Let's go upstairs and explore the wonders of that marvelous sunken bathtub I saw a few weeks back."

His brow shot up. "You're not tired of water yet?"

Green eyes twinkling, she replied, "Who said anything about water?"

THEY MADE LOVE in his huge king-size bed for what seemed like hours. Three hours to be exact. The brass clock on the mantel had just gonged midnight, the fire in the hearth long since fading to embers.

Adam leaned over and gently brushed the side of Meredith's face with the back of his fingertips, marveling at her beauty and at how deeply she had affected him. He wasn't sure, now that he'd had a taste of her, he would be able to let her go. The provocative thought disturbed him.

"I promised you dinner. Are you still game?"

Meredith turned her face into his hand and kissed his palm, wondering if she'd ever be the same again. Tonight had been a magical fairy tale. She was Cinderella to Adam's Prince Charming. But would she live happily ever after? That was the question.

Pushing away thoughts better left unexplored, she replied with a teasing grin, "I don't know about you, but I've worked up quite an appetite."

His grin was achingly sexy. "Famished. Absolutely."

They were out of bed and down the stairs in a matter of moments, giggling like a couple of schoolkids, and still buck naked when they entered the kitchen.

"I've never dined in the buff before," Meredith confessed, perching herself on a stool at the counter, quite shocked at her own behavior. She'd done quite a few things tonight she'd never done before…or as well.

Opening the refrigerator, he stuck his head inside. "I can make a decent omelet. How's that sound?" He hadn't cooked in years, but he was pretty sure he could still do it. If not, there was always pizza delivery.

"Yummy. Do you need any help?"

He moved to the long, gray granite counter, basket of eggs in hand. "Though your luscious breasts are a bit of a distraction, I think I can manage." He grinned when her cheeks turned bright pink and reached for a hunk of cheddar.

Eyeing the paper towels, she wondered how many she'd need to wrap herself up like a mummy. "Perhaps I should get dressed. I wouldn't want you to injure yourself."

"I cook naked all the time," he lied. "Never had any problems. And I think you're worth the risk, at any rate."

"Flatterer," she quipped, but her heart was beating double time. "Doesn't Mrs. Fishburn mind you messing up her kitchen?" The gray-haired woman didn't look like someone who would allow such flamboyant behavior. She'd never seen Helen Fishburn with a hair out of place. The taut bun she wore was always firmly anchored at the back of her neck, and there'd never been so much as a smudge on her pristine, white apron.

For someone used to wiping her hands on what was at hand, including whatever she was wearing at the moment, Meredith found the housekeeper's restraint quite astonishing.

"The old gal would be totally mortified if she knew someone was parading about naked in her kitchen," Adam replied, eyes twinkling. "I'd probably get spanked with a wooden spoon. Mrs. Fishburn is rather obsessive about germs. I'm sure the sight of naked skin would send her right over the edge."

It was difficult to picture staid Mrs. Fishburn in such an outlandish situation, so Meredith changed the subject. "Remember that day we went to the park and I went upstairs to change?"

"I do. You wore that sexy jogging outfit, as I recall." Ignoring her surprise that he'd remembered such a trivial detail, he shoved a blue Wedgwood plate and silver fork in front of her, then sat down on the stool next to her. "Why?"

Taking a bite of her omelet, then another, she murmured approvingly. "This is wonderful. How'd you know I loved mushrooms?"

"Just a guess. So what's so interesting upstairs? Besides the bedroom, that is?" Like a dastardly villain in a melodrama, he wiggled his brows at her, twirling the ends of an imaginary mustache.

"Behave yourself," she said with a laugh. "I noticed a room that contained a huge model train set and wondered if it was yours." She knew it was, from what Andrew had previously told her, and wondered why Adam chose to keep it such a secret.

He was about to deny it, fearing she'd think his love of model trains childish, as his father had, but he couldn't bring himself to lie. "Yes. The trains are mine. I'm sure you think it's silly for a grown man to play with trains, but—"

She shook her head. "Not at all. I think it's quite charming. I used to collect dolls when I was a kid. I still have most of my Barbie collection."

"You don't. I mean, you do?" Relief bubbled up inside of him. "Would you like to see my trains?" He smiled a rueful smile. "I guess most men would ask a woman to see their etchings, not their toy trains."

But then Adam Morgan wasn't most men, Meredith thought.

"If they're as cute as the caboose I've already taken a gander at, I know I'm going to be quite the model train enthusiast."

MEREDITH awoke the following morning with two thoughts in her head: she'd had unprotected sex in the pool for the first time in her life, which had been totally stupid, not to mention dangerous, and she was in love. Which was even dumber! And possibly more dangerous.

She couldn't be in love with Adam Morgan. It was ridiculous to think a relationship between them could work. Sure, he'd let her wear his engineer's hat, had even allowed her to run the trains around the track a few times. And even if she'd been the first to enter his inner sanctum, as he'd confessed, that didn't mean there weren't a multitude of problems to face.

They were just two different types of people. He was rich, for starters. Wealthy. Educated. Used to the finer things in life. His silverware and china even matched!

She was not in the same class. No way. Not even close. They weren't social equals and never would be.

Her father had died as a result of working in the Morgan coal mines. And her mother would likely perish on the spot if she found out Meredith had fallen in love with her worst enemy.

Glancing at the sleeping man beside her, Meredith felt tears well up behind her lids. She loved Adam, had been hired to find him a woman to wed—a suitable woman—and as much as she wished it were otherwise, it just wouldn't be her.

Not that he was asking!

Chapter Ten

"Marry me."

Eyes wide open, Adam was grinning at her like some comedian who'd just told the funniest joke in the world.

Only Meredith wasn't laughing.

Pulling the covers up to her chin, she leaned back against the down pillows, trying her damnedest not to cry. "Very funny." The man had a warped sense of humor, that was for certain.

He rolled toward her, taking her hand in his, kissing the inside of her wrist and eliciting an instantaneous heart-pounding, primal response that made her want to curse herself. And him.

"Don't you see? It's perfect. I need a wife, and you're not engaged to anyone else that I know of. I mean—I assume you wouldn't have slept with me if you were. And it would solve a great many problems."

For whom? she wanted to ask.

Pulling her hand out of his, she eased herself out of bed, grabbing a blanket as she did, and wrapped it around herself. She wished she could cloak her heart as easily, but she knew it was too late for that.

"I thought you were certifiable when I first met you, Adam, but now I'm sure of it. I have no intention of marrying you."

Eyes rounding to silver dollars, he seemed astounded by her refusal. She doubted the man had been refused much in his lifetime. Hadn't she acquiesced to every delicious thing he'd suggested last night? Just thinking about what they'd done in that big playground of a bed made heat rise to her cheeks.

Adam was a very inventive lover; she'd been a very willing and enthusiastic pupil. If Morgantown Senior High had had sex education with Adam Morgan as part of their curriculum, she would have earned an A+ for sure.

"But—"

"And no, I wouldn't have made love with you had I been engaged to someone else," she interrupted, green eyes flashing. "How could you even think it? I might be a great many things—" stupid, came to mind "—but I'm not disloyal or dishonorable." She turned about quickly so he couldn't see the tears threatening to fall.

"You're not being at all practical about my offer, Meredith. I can offer you the world, anything your heart desires. You could travel to exotic places, redecorate the house and shop to your heart's content." Women loved doing that, he knew.

Taking a deep breath, she turned back to face him. Her heart was breaking, but she wouldn't give him the satisfaction of knowing. "You are obviously unaware that money can't buy happiness, Adam. Or a wife, for that matter. I will not marry for the sake of convenience or to fatten my bank account, which admittedly needs fattening. I'll only marry for love.

And I'll only marry someone who loves me back. I'm just selfish enough to want to be the center of my husband's world, not some *business merger.*" The words dripped with contempt.

"Isn't that how you phrased it when we first met, Adam—a business merger?" And she had responded by asking, "What's love got to do with it?" Now she had her answer: nothing. Nothing at all.

Adam wasn't sure if he was in love with Meredith. The emotion was totally alien to him. But what he did know was that Meredith was the first woman he'd ever made love to that he wanted to wake up with in the morning, the first woman he found interesting, stimulating, incredibly desirable and who would make a wonderful mother for Megan and Andrew.

Her enthusiasm for model trains was just an added bonus.

"I shouldn't have declared myself so abruptly," he said, moving to stand before her, totally unaware of how his nakedness was affecting her. "You obviously need time to think about what I'm offering." Once she had, he was sure she would come around to his way of thinking. After all, his suggestion was exceedingly logical, practical.

And what was wrong with a sound business merger? He'd helped build Morgan Coal Mining and Manufacturing on just such principles.

Her sigh was filled with disappointment. "You're the one who needs to think things through, Adam. You need to start thinking with your emotions, your heart." She patted his chest, fighting the urge to explore the thick mat of hair, fisting her fingers instead. "Your heart, not your brain."

Adam's bland expression gave no clue as to what he was thinking, and Meredith wasn't sure if what she'd said had made any impression. But she forged ahead, anyway, figuring she had nothing to lose but his business. She'd already lost her heart. "Your plan to find a wife by way of a media search is a prime example of your lack of understanding of the human condition. Romance and love are what women want, not material possessions."

He began to protest, but she held up her hand, cutting him off. "Oh, I'm sure you can find a multitude of women who would jump at the chance to marry you for your money. But are they going to love you? Are they going to be there for the long haul?

"And what kind of mother will they make for your niece and nephew? Megan and Andrew have already been devastated by the loss of their mother and father. To stick them with some money-grabbing, cliché of a stepmother is cruel beyond imagination. Or hadn't you considered *them* in your grand scheme of things?"

Grabbing his robe, he shrugged it on, knotting the belt with an impatient tug, while dark storm clouds gathered in the depths of his silvery eyes. "Megan and Andrew are my primary consideration. I want what's best for them. I always have." And he would deny it to the death if anyone said otherwise.

"I'll do my best to find you a suitable wife, Adam." *Even if it kills me.* "But what happened between us last night will not be repeated. It was wonderful, but it was definitely a big mistake. It won't happen again. Mixing business and pleasure never works out, as I'm sure you know."

He opened his mouth to speak, then thought better of it, unable to dispute the logic of her reasoning, unwilling to interpret what was in his heart.

"Now if you'll excuse me," she said, "I'm late for work." Grabbing her dress and underclothing, Meredith took refuge in the bathroom where she proceeded to cry her eyes out.

Fully composed in less than five minutes, she had dressed and departed without so much as a goodbye peck on the cheek, leaving Adam with a feeling of loss he'd only experienced once before—the day his sister died.

He still missed Allison. Not a day went by when he didn't think about her and all the good times they'd shared as children. He'd loved her a great deal. They'd always been there for each other, offering comfort and emotional support whenever being a Morgan became too much to handle.

His sister's death served as a painful reminder that attaching oneself to another human being meant opening oneself up to a world of hurt.

Adam was hurting right now—Meredith was to blame—and he didn't like the feeling one little bit.

THROUGH THE POWERFUL binoculars, Tremayne's gaze fixed intently on the attractive redhead who had just emerged from the mansion. She looked upset, but definitely sated.

Morgan hadn't wasted any time bedding his new wedding coordinator, Curtis thought, recognizing the woman from her photo in the newspaper. Not that he could blame him. The man always did have impeccable taste, and she was definitely a knockout. Buxom, long legs—a body just made for sin.

He felt a need too long denied well up inside him like a geyser. He hadn't been with a woman since his wife, and that felt like a lifetime ago.

Not that Allison had ever been all that satisfying in the sack. Far from it. She'd had too many repressed feelings, too much self-conscious garbage to contend with, probably inherited from her cold-as-a-fish mother. "Lilah, the Lizard," Curtis had pegged the Morgan matriarch.

Since Allison had proven to be such a big disappointment in bed, he'd been forced to take his pleasure elsewhere to make up for her lack of inventiveness and unwillingness to satisfy him.

He liked his sex hot and hard. And he sure had a taste for well-built redheads with legs that didn't quit.

Jotting down the time of Meredith Baxter's departure in his notebook, he set down his binoculars and pulled a cigarette from his shirt pocket. He'd been watching the Morgan household for weeks, noting departure and arrival times of the various employees, the kids' school schedules and all of the many visits the Baxter woman had made to the mansion.

If Morgan had screwed her on each of those occasions, he was one lucky SOB. Another reason to revenge himself on the wealthy bastard.

Proper planning made for successful execution. He'd learned that from the Morgans themselves, especially the old man, who'd been a stickler for details. How fitting he'd now be able to turn their own methods against them.

Revenge was going to be sweet. And very lucrative. Very lucrative, indeed.

"WHO DIED?"

Randall's question hit Meredith right between the

eyes as she stepped through the door of the bridal salon, hoping to avoid answering any questions about her lackluster appearance. But of course Randall, being Randall never let appearances slide.

"You look like doo-doo, sweetie, if you don't mind my saying so."

Self-consciously she brushed at her hair, which was curling riotously because she hadn't had time to blow-dry it, and straightened her skirt, hating to admit that she felt like something that belonged on the bottom of a shoe.

She'd gone home to shower after leaving Adam's house, hoping she'd be able to cleanse herself of the need to be with him, but it hadn't worked. She felt just as needy as ever, only now she was also a candidate for St. John's Wort.

She'd never had a broken heart before—maybe a few minor cracks, but not the major fissure now existing in her chest—and she wasn't sure how long it would take for it to mend. If it ever did. Right now that didn't seem likely.

"I'm fine, Randall. I'm sorry I'm late, but I... I overslept." She hated lying, but it was nobody's business what had transpired between her and Adam. She didn't want to think about it. It was history, a mistake, an unfortunate lapse of judgment.

But Meredith had been thinking about it, and she felt devastated that Adam didn't love her.

"Judging from those dark circles under your eyes, you must have had an exhausting night." His right brow arched knowingly. "By the way, your mother called asking why you didn't drop by the nursing home to see her last night."

Meredith's face paled. "Oh, no! Was she very upset? I had so much to do last night that I completely forgot to call her." Damn Adam! The man had made her forget about her own mother. Okay, so her hormones may have played a small part, but it was definitely Adam's fault for making them rage out of control.

"I'll call her, explain what happened, then drop by and visit her later."

"She asked if you were with Morgan. I covered for you and said no, but we both know that's a lie."

"I hate it when you interrogate me, Randall. Just because you're in law school doesn't give you the right—"

He draped his arm around her shoulder and squeezed gently. "It's more about being your friend than about being a lawyer, sweetie. You know I care for you. I don't want to see you get hurt."

She heaved a sigh. "Too late for that, counselor."

"What happened?" But the expression on her face was telling, and Randall merely shook his head. "*Sacrebleu!* You slept with him, didn't you?"

"That's none of your business. But yes, I did." What was the point of lying? She and Randall had never kept any secrets from each other. Besides, he'd wheedle it out of her eventually, ply her with cookies and Godiva chocolates until she gave in.

Weakness, thy name is Meredith.

"*Mon dieu.*"

"Tell me about it. Adam Morgan's asked me to marry him."

"What!" His bright blue eyes rounded, nearly bulging from their sockets.

"He thinks I'm the perfect candidate to be his

bride. I fit all the nauseating qualifications. And the kids like me. There was no mention of the *L* word, however.''

Randall pushed Meredith into a chair at the table, saying, ''Fortunately I had the foresight to pick up a turtle praline cheesecake from Lovett's Bakery this morning. I think it's time to break it open.''

She shook her head. ''I couldn't. I'm too upset to eat right now. Maybe later?'' She forced a small smile at his thoughtfulness, then said, ''By the way, where's Sally? I hope she's not ill.'' She needed the woman to videotape the three applicants who were coming in later today. Because of what had transpired this morning, she intended to step up her pace in finding Adam a bride—one other than herself.

''No, sweetie. Sally's feeling just fine these days, due, I suspect, to the attentions of a certain handsome attorney who keeps dropping by and taking her to lunch. She's at the bank making a deposit and should be back any moment.''

The front door opened and they turned, but it wasn't Sally who entered; it was the delivery man from Kramer's Florist, who was pushing a handcart loaded with roses in every color imaginable. ''Where do you want 'em, Meredith? I've got more in the truck to bring in.''

Her mouth dropped open as she viewed the opulent and very expensive arrangements. The scent they emitted was sickeningly sweet, almost cloying. ''There must be some mistake. I didn't order any flowers. The next wedding isn't until two weeks from Saturday, and Annie Garrett ordered carnations, stephanotis and baby's breath, not roses.''

''It's beginning to smell like a funeral parlor in

here," Randall noted, wrinkling his nose in disgust. "I suggest you read the card and see who your admire is, as if we didn't already know."

Her heart sank. She'd made it perfectly clear to Adam that from here on out it was going to be strictly business between them. The card indicated differently: Marry me. I won't take no for an answer.

She gritted her teeth. Adam's persistence, not to mention his obtuseness, annoyed the heck out of her. "Don't bring the other cart in, Harold," she shouted to the driver from the doorway, who'd gone back to his van. "Take the rest of the order to the hospital and have the flowers distributed among the patients. I don't have room for them here."

"Will do. But I don't think this'll be the last of the deliveries. I heard Mrs. Kramer say that there was a standing order."

"Good Lord!" *Was the man insane?*

"You sure must have impressed some fella, Meredith. We ain't had such a large order since Allistair Morgan died."

"Apparently the Morgans are known for their excesses, Harold," she said with no small amount of sarcasm, thanking the balding driver, then shutting the door and slumping onto the chair.

A few moments later Sally walked in and, upon noticing the large array of flowers, asked, "Are any of these for me?" a hopeful expression crossing her face.

Randall smiled apologetically. "No, sweet Sally, they're all for Meredith. Apparently, she's made her bed and now has to lie in it. The good news is it'll be strewn with rose petals."

Meredith flashed the man a look of pure annoyance. "You can be replaced."

"Then you'd have no one to share your passion for chocolate with. You know Sally doesn't have nearly the sweet tooth I do."

"Maybe I'd lose weight."

"Why do I feel like I've just entered the Twilight Zone?" Sally asked, tossing her coat on the chair. "What's going on?"

Randall opened his mouth to explain, but Meredith beat him to the punch, relating the gist of recent events, including Adam's marriage proposal.

"Mr. Morgan wants to marry you? But that's wonderful! Isn't it?" she added, noting her employer's deep frown.

"Under normal circumstances I suppose it would be. But Adam doesn't love me, and I won't settle for anything but the genuine article."

"You're in love with him, aren't you?"

Sally's question hung in the air like humidity on a hot summer day, making Meredith feel very uncomfortable, the chasm in her chest widening another inch. Finally she said, "Yes, I am, totally and insanely."

"Mon dieu!" Randall clasped his hand over his heart, then threw in a *sacrebleu* for good measure.

"But that doesn't matter," Meredith went on, ignoring the man's theatrics. "One-sided relationships never work out. Adam's made it crystal clear that he doesn't love me."

"He told you that?" the blond woman asked.

"Well, no. Not in so many words. But he didn't make any heartfelt declarations either, so—"

"Sweetie, men are much more reticent than

women about sharing their feelings. And perhaps he just doesn't know what's in his heart. I've had similar relationships, and if you give him time—''

She shook her head. "Time is something I don't have, Randall. We've only a few weeks left to find Adam Morgan a bride, which is exactly what we're going to do.

"I've already spent his deposit, and I need the balance of the money he's going to pay us when the wedding is done to keep this business afloat. So I suggest we get to work and sort through the rest of the applications.''

Her heart would mend in time. It had to.

Sally stepped forward and wrapped her arms about her friend's waist. "I'm sorry. I wish there was something I could do.''

A steely glint of determination entered Meredith's eyes. "There is. Help me find Adam a bride. The sooner he's married, the sooner I can get my life back to normal.''

Normal, however, was very highly overrated, in her opinion.

Chapter Eleven

Adam's intercom buzzed, but he didn't need to answer it to know what his secretary Grace Mulrooney, was going to tell him. Gifts he'd sent to Meredith had been arriving back at his office most of the afternoon, unopened and marked Return to Sender.

Meredith was determined to reject his marriage proposal. He, on the other hand, was just as determined to marry her. It was the perfect solution for everyone involved. And when it came to determination there were few who could best him.

Pressing down on the phone's intercom button, he asked, "Yes, Grace, what is it?" then waited for the usual response.

There was an embarrassed silence before the woman said, "What would you like me to do with the gifts, Mr. Morgan? All of the jewelry has been returned, as has the set of matching luggage, the airline tickets to Europe and the gold-plated, engraved dog collar."

Adam's brow shot up at that. He thought surely the present for Harrison would have weakened Meredith a bit. He knew how much she loved that dog. "Just stack them up in the corner with the others. I intend to deliver the gifts in person. I think I'll have better results.''

His secretary's voice held a definite lack of confidence when she replied, "I... I hope so, Mr. Morgan.''

Grace still insisted on calling him Mr. Morgan, though he'd given her leave to address him as Adam years ago. But she was a stickler for propriety, had never addressed the old man as Allistair, and she wasn't about to overstep her bounds by addressing his son in such a familiar way.

"Was there something you wished to add, Grace? If so, just spit it out. You've worked for me long enough to know that I welcome divergent opinions.'' The intercom suddenly went silent, then the door to his office opened, and the older woman with the graying blond hair stepped in.

An attractive woman in her early sixties, Grace Mulrooney took as much care with her appearance as she did with Adam's correspondence. A motherly sort, she'd worked for the Morgans for over twenty years, was efficient and well organized, typed seventy words per minute, took dictation—a rarity these days—and was someone who only offered advice if you pulled it out of her—another rarity.

The secretary smiled tentatively, her blue eyes kind behind tortoiseshell glasses. "Some women don't respond well to presents, Mr. Morgan. I've met Miss Baxter. She seems to be a very single-minded person. I'm not sure overwhelming her with flowers and gifts is the best way to woo her.''

"Nonsense. Women love flowers. And what woman wouldn't love to travel and have expensive jewelry thrust at her?''

"It seems the woman you've singled out, Mr. Morgan," she reminded him, clearly wanting to say more, but not daring to overstep her bounds. "Perhaps you should consider a softer approach."

"Softer?" His forehead wrinkled at the suggestion. "In what way? I'm used to taking the direct approach, Grace. You know that. I hate pussyfooting around. In matters of business—"

"This isn't business, Mr. Morgan. It's a matter of the heart."

Funny, Meredith had said something very similar. Adam released a sigh. He didn't profess to understand women, which is probably why he'd remained a bachelor for so long. Delving into the female mind was like walking barefoot through a minefield. There was just no telling what one might step in and what might get shot off.

The older woman looked extremely nervous for having spoken her mind and Adam tendered a reassuring smile. "I'll give your suggestion some thought, Grace. Thanks." She took the dismissal without further comment and closed the door quietly as she left, the familiar fragrance of her perfume lingering behind like sunshine on a bed of roses.

Leaning back in his chair, the soft leather creaking in response, Adam put his feet up on the windowsill, stared out at the historic city and reached for the jar of sunflower seeds Grace thoughtfully kept filled on his desk.

With its substantial old brick and stone buildings and tree-lined thoroughfares, Morgantown was a city of contrasts—old and new, brick and steel. What had started as a small, residential community on the banks of the Monongahela River had evolved into a bustling industrial city, thanks, in part, to his family's coal mining and manufacturing business.

His ancestor Colonel Zackquill Morgan had founded Morgantown back in 1766, and there'd been Morgans presiding over the city in one capacity or another ever since.

Coal had made the Morgans extremely wealthy, and they in turn had repaid in kind by helping to transform the blue-collar community into a well-respected university mecca. West Virginia University was now the heart and soul of the area, and the largest employer.

A robin trilled on a branch outside the window; the sun shone brightly, as if to defy Adam's thunderous mood; but he took no pleasure in it, the warmer weather or much of anything else.

Since the night they'd made love four days ago, he couldn't get Meredith out of his mind. He wanted to be with her, kiss her and make love to her until they were both exhausted and numbed from the experience.

He wanted to marry her.

He wanted to hear her sighs of pleasure when they made love, her gentle snores while she slept. He wanted her face to be the first thing he saw upon awakening in the morning and the last thing he gazed upon when going to sleep at night.

He wanted her in his life forever.

Why couldn't that be enough? Why did women always talk of love and hearts and flowers, as if that was all that was important in a relationship? What about mutual interests, respect, friendship, laughter? They had all that.

Allison had been madly in love with Curtis Tremayne, and where had that gotten her? A cold slab of steel in a morgue, a coffin six feet under, that's where.

Love was highly overrated, in his opinion. It was extremely doubtful that his father had been madly in love with his mother. Theirs had been a marriage of opportunity, not a union of the heart, but they'd gotten along well for almost forty years before his death. True, the old man had had his share of affairs that no one ever spoke about, but that didn't mean he didn't care for Lilah in his own way.

His mother had seemed contented enough. She'd shopped until her cavernous closets were filled with designer creations, surrounded herself with influential people, who were more concerned with appearances and pedigree than content, and traveled numerous times to the far reaches of the world.

Her behavior had always seemed so exceedingly self-absorbed to Adam. But perhaps that had been to cover up her unhappiness. He'd never really thought about it until now, had never pondered why his mother had been so remote, so happy with superficial trappings and unhappy with her home life and children.

Could her actions have been devices to protect herself from the emptiness she felt inside, from the humiliation her husband had heaped upon her by choosing younger women over her?

Adam didn't know the answers. Man-woman relationships were just so damn complicated, which is why he'd always shied away from them. The sex was great, but the rest of the emotional entanglements got in the way of a perfectly good alliance. There was something to be said for detachment, he'd decided.

Morgan men are not demonstrative, his father had always said to him, as if to explain his lack of affection toward his children and wife.

And maybe the old man had been right. It had always been difficult for Adam to express his emotions and deep-seated feelings. He tended to pull back when people got too close, too far into his comfort zone. Successful relationships outside of business had never been easy for him. Peter was his one and only true friend, and only because Peter had taken the initiative and would never take no for an answer.

Now Adam was behaving the same way with Meredith—unable to take no for an answer, but unable to allow her inside, where she wanted to be.

Meredith believed in happily ever after, which is why she read those sappy romance novels and chose to plan other peoples' weddings. But Adam knew that, though happy endings might take place in a book, they didn't exist in the real world, in the here and now. He'd seen firsthand too many unhappy relationships, supposedly based on love, flounder then die, and he wasn't buying into the myth.

"WHAT IS IT, Meredith? What's wrong? You haven't seemed yourself these past few days. Is there something going on at work you haven't told me about?"

Meredith heaved a deep sigh at her mother's questions, cursing inwardly her perceptiveness in reading her so well. There was no way she could confide in the older woman about her problems with Adam. Her mother would offer no sympathy, no shoulder to cry on, and Meredith just wasn't up to a lecture these days. Fighting off Adam's pursuit was hard enough to handle without listening to her mother's well-meaning, though skewed, advice.

"I'm having difficulty with the Morgan wedding, that's all," she explained, ignoring her mother's pinched expression at the mention of her adversary's name. "The man is impossible to please. I found him three excellent bridal candidates and he's dismissed them without plausible explanation."

The women she'd singled out had been exquisite. Breathtakingly beautiful, with figures that could rival any movie starlet, two held Masters degrees, while a third boasted a golf score of seventy-five, and all were able to converse on a variety of subjects.

Though it had been difficult for Meredith to offer them up, knowing how perfectly suitable they were for Adam, she'd done so, anyway, because he needed a bride and because she wasn't going to accept his proposal, no matter how many gifts and flowers he sent or how many times he asked—make that demanded—that she marry him.

Louise tsked and shook her head. "I told you that man was trouble. Rich people are peculiar. They've got strange ways."

"Yes, that may be true," Meredith agreed with a sigh, "but I needed the money. And I still have to fulfill my obligation of finding Adam a bride." *And if you knew who Adam had set his sights on, you'd be peeling yourself off the ceiling.*

Hesitating, and looking decidedly uncomfortable with what she was about to say, Louise's cheeks filled with color. "Well, Merry, I don't normally talk about such things, because you're still young and…well, I'm just not comfortable with all this liberated type of nonsense, but— But some men don't like women. They prefer—''

''Mother!'' Meredith's voice held all of the mortification she felt. ''Adam Morgan is definitely not of that persuasion.'' And she wasn't about to reveal how she knew that for a fact.

She quickly changed the subject. ''Nurse Mullins said the doctor was here today. Are you sick? I hope you're not keeping things from me.''

''It was just routine, honey. Dr. Carpenter said my condition has deteriorated a bit, but nothing unexpected, and certainly nothing to be alarmed about.''

Meredith reached out to take her mother's hand. It was cold and clammy, another indication of her declining condition. She voiced the thoughts plaguing her conscience of late. ''Perhaps I should sell the business, Mom. Maybe I would make enough money to—''

''Stop talking nonsense, Meredith! You'll do no such thing. We've discussed this before, and I've told you repeatedly that I've accepted the fact I'm going to die. I'll not have you tossing away your only form of livelihood in some unselfish effort to prolong the inevitable.''

Meredith blanched at the harsh reality of her mother's words. Louise had always been more honest with herself and others than Meredith could ever hope to be. She was a realist while Meredith clung to her optimism like a lifeline. ''Mom, please—''

Louise's militant expression changed suddenly, and she smiled softly, patting her daughter's cheek. ''No one lives forever, Merry. That's just the way things are.''

''But if I could have afforded to pay for a heart

transplant... I feel so helpless, so responsible that I couldn't do more to help you."

"Please stop that kind of talk, honey. I won't stand for you berating yourself. You've done all you could. And though I may not always seem grateful, I am. More than you'll ever know.

"I've made my peace with God and with myself. And so should you."

MEREDITH WAS STILL BROODING over her mother's words a short time later when the kitchen phone rang. She'd gone home to a cold dinner of ham sandwiches and chips, and she wasn't in the mood to talk to anyone, especially Adam.

So, she was both surprised and relieved to hear "Hi, Meredith! It's me, Megan," when she finally answered.

Relieved, yes, but suspicious nonetheless. A warning bell sounded loud and clear; Megan had never called her before. "Hello, sweetie. What can I do for you?"

"Well, Uncle— Ouch! Stop that, Andrew. Me and Andrew were wondering if you could come over for dinner tomorrow night. We wanted to have a sleepover."

A sleepover! Now she knew for certain Adam was behind the child's call. "As much as I'd like to see you and Andrew, sweetie—" she purposely left out mentioning Adam, hoping he was listening in "—I have plans for tomorrow evening."

"You do?" Silence, then "Hold on, okay?" A muffled sound ensued, followed by a series of whispers, then Megan came back on the line and said,

''Can't you cancel them? Me and Andrew really, really want to see you. It's im-imperatif.''

Imperative! As if a six-year-old child would actually say such a word. *Oh, Adam, your denseness is showing again.* Meredith smiled wickedly to herself. ''I've got a date, sweetie. Someone I met at the nursing home.''

She could hear Adam's strangled ''The nursing home! My God!'' and her smile widened.

''I probably shouldn't be telling you this, Megan, since you're so young and all, but the man I met makes my blood boil, and I get this funny tingling in my toes whenever he walks into—''

In the background she heard a loud bellow. Then Megan said urgently, ''I gotta go now, Meredith. Uncle Adam wants to talk to you. Bye.''

Before she could refuse, Adam's deep voice filled her ear, and her blood did start to boil, and her toes did indeed begin to tingle, as did a few other places.

''I don't believe for a second, Meredith, that you are actually going out with a male nurse. Now stop this nonsense and marry me.''

Meredith tried to keep her temper under control, though Adam's imperious tone grated her composure. ''Using Megan and Andrew to lure me back into your bed is not going to work, Adam. I told you before and I'm telling you again that I won't marry a man who doesn't love me.''

There was an uncomfortable silence, then ''I... I like you a lot. Doesn't that count for anything?''

She should have been flattered. She doubted Adam liked that many people. But under the present circumstances she didn't feel at all charitable and said, ''It might, if I were a cocker spaniel.''

"You are being totally obstinate and unreasonable. I am offering you the world, which is a far greater commodity than my heart."

"I'm beginning to think you don't have a heart, Adam, which is really too bad, because I would never marry a man without one. I realize your upbringing has left you with issues that only you can resolve, and I'm sorry for that. But I won't spend the rest of my life with a man who's passion for model trains and sunflower seeds exceeds his passion for me."

"Meredith."

There was a great deal of pain in that one word, but she chose to ignore it. "And please don't keep sending me gifts and flowers. I'm sure you realize by now that material things are not going to change my mind about marrying you." Though the tickets to Europe had given her pause, for about fifteen seconds.

"But I can't stop thinking about you," he admitted, and Meredith's heart began fluttering strangely, though she did her best to ignore that, too.

"Soon you'll have a new wife to focus your attention on. I suggest you stop being so picky and choose one of the women I've presented."

"None were acceptable."

"I'm running out of candidates, and you're running out of time, Adam. You need to take action. Make a decision."

"I've made my decision."

She bit her lip, dreading to hear who he had chosen. Was it the blonde with the porcelain complexion—not a freckle in sight on that one—or the golf enthusiast with the long legs that didn't quit? Either one would make him an ideal wife.

"Great!" she said with far more enthusiasm than she felt. "Which one's it going to be?"

"You."

And then he slammed down the phone before she could scream vile names at him.

Chapter Twelve

Despite Meredith's adamant refusal to marry him, Adam was not about to give up. If gifts and flowers wouldn't soften her, if Megan's sweet pleas couldn't get a rise out of the stubborn woman, then Adam had no recourse but to visit the nursing home—and at the same time check out this male nurse Meredith supposedly had a date with—and enlist the aid of her mother, who, he hoped, had more common sense than her daughter.

The following morning found him in Louise Baxter's suite of rooms at the Pleasant Acres Nursing Home, but there was nothing pleasant about the look the woman was directing at him from her chair by the window. The reception was so chilly he could have frozen TV dinners without refrigeration.

"How dare you come here, Mr. Morgan! You've got gall, I'll give you that." She crossed her arms over her chest and stared out the window, hoping he'd take the hint and leave.

Adam was used to dealing with prickly competitors and antagonistic business associates, but he'd never felt the out-and-out hostility—borderline hatred—that was being bulleted at him by Meredith's mother.

Did the older woman know of his and Meredith's intimate relationship? It seemed highly unlikely that a grown woman would confess such a thing to her mother. Or was Mrs. Baxter fearful he had used and intended to discard her only daughter?

Seating himself on the love seat nearby, he intended to set the record straight, ease her mind a bit. "Mrs. Baxter," he began, "let me assure you I have only Meredith's best interest at heart. I plan to marry her, and I was hoping to gain your support in my efforts to do so. You see, Meredith isn't wholly enamored with the idea, and I thought you might—"

Her head jerked around so quickly, her lips twisted so menacingly, Adam thought he might be viewing a showing of *The Exorcist*. The devil definitely had a hold of Louise Baxter at the moment.

"Are you out of your mind, Mr. Morgan, or just so damn arrogant that you think you're the catch of the day? You are the last man I would ever want my daughter to marry. I don't care how much money your family has. Your father was an unfeeling despot who allowed his employees to work in unsafe and unsanitary conditions. My husband Henry died working for your precious company. I'll not sacrifice my daughter, as well."

Adam's mouth dropped open. He had no idea Meredith's father had worked for Morgan Coal Mining. Why hadn't she ever mentioned it? The news apparently accounted for the inhospitable reception he'd received from her mother, and was quite possibly the reason Meredith was so hesitant to marry him. "I'm sorry, Mrs. Baxter. I didn't know."

She seemed taken aback by the admission, but only momentarily. "Meredith didn't tell you about Henry's death?"

He shook his head, his sweaty palms pressing down on his thighs. "No. I'm sorry. If I'd known—"

Her laugh was caustic enough to eat through metal. "You'd do what, Mr. Morgan? Even your money can't bring back the dead."

Adam felt his cheeks warm—something totally out of character for him. But then, he'd never conversed with Satan's handmaiden before. Reeling in his anger, he said, "I meant—"

She cut him off again. "My husband died of black lung disease, but Henry died long before the ailment finally took him. A man who loses his ability to work and support his family, who's lost his pride and manhood, has no reason to live. Leastways, that's how Henry looked at it.

"Your company never provided my husband with any benefits beyond the paltry allotment he received from the union, which was barely enough to bury him. Your father could have helped us survive, Mr. Morgan. Helped us and countless others like us who lived their lives in shame and squalor because Morgan Coal was a cold, heartless employer who just didn't give a tinker's damn."

"Mrs. Baxter, please." He held out his hands beseechingly, vowing silently to get to the bottom of her accusations. Morgans had always treated their employees well, certainly with respect and consideration. Maybe not like family, but better than most, and Adam didn't understand what could've possibly happened to Henry Baxter.

"No, I will not help to convince my daughter to

marry you, Mr. Morgan. If Meredith's refused you, then I credit her with having good sense. Obviously, she's aware of the kind of man you are. The kind of man your father was."

Adam's expression congested, and his voice turned cold. He'd spent his whole life avoiding comparisons with his father, and he wasn't about to allow a bitter, old woman to start now. "I'm nothing like my father, Mrs. Baxter. You don't know me, don't know anything about me. It's wrong of you to prejudge who I am because of some alleged wrong my father may have done to your family.

"It's always been the policy of Morgan Coal Mining and Manufacturing to look out for their employees, and the same was true under my father's direction. I don't know why Mr. Baxter was treated in such an uncaring fashion, but you have my word that I will find out." He stood to leave.

She snorted derisively. "The word of a Morgan is no word at all. I've said all I have to say on the matter." Crossing her arms over her chest once again, she turned her back on him and returned to gazing out the window at a pair of frolicking squirrels, though the sight did not bring her the joy it usually did.

Adam's expression grew more determined. "But I haven't. Not on this matter, or the one I came here originally to discuss with you. We shall meet again, Mrs. Baxter. You have my word on it. And be assured that my word is my bond."

THE FIRST THING ADAM DID upon returning to his office was to call the personnel manager of his company and request the employment files of Henry Baxter.

What he found after going through the man's records was that Louise Baxter had been technically correct. Henry Baxter had fallen ill to black lung disease. The conditions in the mine at the time of his employment had been deplorable, though in keeping with the standard working practices of the day. And he had not been given any monetary support from the Miner's Pension Relief Fund to help allay his medical expenses and supplement his meager union stipend.

There were no notations on the records as to why this was so, and the employment manager at that time—a Michael Keebler—had long since died. He made a note to research the other personnel files of the same time period to see if any other infractions had been committed, and to investigate Keebler's background to learn if he harbored any personal animosity toward Henry Baxter or any of the other miners. They had zero tolerance for such things at MMM.

Adam was extremely upset. To have such a thing happen to any of his workers was unconscionable, to have it happen to Meredith's father—

God, how she must despise me!

Peter walked in at that moment and pulled up short at the look of despair on his friend's face. Growing immediately concerned, he asked, "What's happened? Has there been an accident at one of the mines? Why didn't you call me?"

Sighing deeply, Adam ran agitated fingers through his hair. "No. There's been no accident. At least, not the kind you're thinking of.'' He handed his lawyer the folder.

"It seems Meredith's father used to work for the company. He died of black lung, and his family suffered horribly because we weren't there for him.''

Peter flipped through the pages, then glanced up at Adam, who was wearing his guilt like an oversize hair shirt. "Henry Baxter obviously slipped through the cracks. You can't take the blame for that, Adam. It was before you took over the day-to-day operations of the company.''

"But the fault remains mine, Peter. Don't you see? I'm head of this corporation. Morgans made money off the sweat of miners like Henry Baxter, who paid the ultimate price for our gain. I can't ignore that or sweep it under the carpet to ease my conscience.''

"I don't believe for one second that Meredith blames you for her father's death, if that's what you're thinking. She doesn't have a vindictive bone in her body.''

"Well her mother sure as hell does. The woman practically spit on me when I went to see her this morning.''

Peter's face colored slightly. "Ah, Sally mentioned something about you not being Meredith's mother's favorite person, but I didn't think it warranted a discussion. Guess I should have known you'd try to win over the old lady.''

"Dammit, Peter! The woman hates my guts. And she's totally against me marrying Meredith. I haven't got a prayer in hell now.''

The news of Adam's proposal to Meredith had surprised the attorney. Though he wasn't at all surprised that the lovely woman had turned him down. And inside out, apparently.

The lawyer smiled to himself. When it came to romancing a woman, Adam didn't have a clue. Give the man a business problem or an intricate puzzle and he could solve it. But a woman... The millionaire was hopeless. Instead of buying him a magnifying glass, Peter should have purchased a bulldozer. Adam was not into subtlety. Sometimes you just had to hit the guy over the head with a two-by-four.

"Louise Baxter's a sick woman, Adam. Very sick, from what Sally tells me. Her heart has deteriorated to the point where only a transplant can save her now. She's probably at odds with everyone these days. I don't think—"

Slumping down into his chair, Adam grabbed the sides of his head in anguish. "I had no idea she was so ill, or I'd never have gone there to see her. It certainly wasn't my intention to upset her in any way, though I'm sure I did. Meredith's going to hate me for this."

"Probably. From what I understand, she's very protective of her mother."

Pulling his gaze from the pink blossoming cherry tree outside his window, he shot Peter a lethal glare, then said, "I want you to contact two or three of the top cardiac surgeons in the country and have them at my house by ten o'clock tomorrow morning."

The lawyer's mouth dropped open. "Tomorrow morning? Are you nuts? That's too short a notice. I can't possibly make the necessary—"

"Just do it. Hire a private jet, if necessary, to bring them here. And have them contact the Pleasant Acres Nursing Home and find out who Louise Baxter's personal physician is. They'll need to review her complete medical records and talk to her doctor about her condition."

"But I have a date with Sally tonight," Peter protested, even as he jotted down notes in his book. "We have reservations at The Glass House Grill."

"Well, you're going to just have to cancel them. Order in Chinese instead. You're good at that, I hear." Adam raised a brow at his friend's perplexed look, then added, "Mrs. Baxter pointed out very succinctly that there wasn't a thing I could do to bring back her husband from the dead. She's right. But there is something I can do to pay back Meredith and her mother for my company's oversight in dealing with their loved one.... I intend to save Louise Baxter's life, whether or not she likes the idea."

Peter couldn't very well argue Adam's motive in wanting to save the woman and not come out looking small and selfish. "Sally's very fond of moo shoo pork," he conceded, evaluating the benefits of an intimate dinner at home and smiling to himself. It was time to take their relationship to the next level, whatever that might be. He only knew what he wanted it to be and hoped Sally wanted the same.

"Don't breathe a word of this to your lady friend or Meredith or anyone else. I suspect Meredith will find out soon enough that I visited her mother, and she's not going to be happy about it, which is why I need those doctors here first thing in the morning."

"Is there anything else? Like perhaps, oh...I don't know...maybe parting the Red Sea, turning water into wine?"

He smiled at his friend's sarcasm. "Yes, actually, there is, now that you mention it. Get me two tickets to the Garth Brooks concert that's going to be held at WVU next month. Meredith's a fan, and I'd like to surprise her with them.''

''Tickets to—'' Peter's eyes widened before his expression grew resigned. ''Never mind. I'm sure I can find some scalper who'll part with them. But it's going to cost you.''

''It always does, Peter. But I'd pay any amount of money to make Meredith happy.''

''Then why don't you just give her the one thing she truly wants, Adam, and it won't cost you a thing?''

The mining mogul popped a handful of sunflower seeds into his mouth, cocking a brow. ''What's that?''

But Peter was already out the door and didn't answer. Adam thought he'd heard him utter ''stupid fool!'' before shutting it behind him, but he couldn't be certain.

SALLY LEANED BACK against the cushions of the comfortable leather sofa and toyed nervously with the cut crystal wineglass in her hand. When Peter had suggested ordering in Chinese and eating dinner at his place, her first reaction had been to say no. But he had been so apologetic about having to cancel their dinner plans, and so frazzled about some project Mr. Morgan had set him to, that she couldn't possibly refuse and add to his misery, not after all the kind things he'd done for her.

While Peter was occupied in his study making phone calls, Sally took several deep breaths and forced herself to relax. His attractive condo overlooking the river was certainly conducive to relaxation. The interior color scheme of hunter and gold was masculine, yet not overbearing. She loved the cherry wood occasional tables, the hand-hooked rugs on the burnished pine floors, and the touches of brass accents in the numerous candlesticks and lamps. The fireplace had been constructed of fieldstone and lent a cozy touch to the room.

Peter had impeccable taste, but that was something she already knew about him. He dressed exceedingly fashionably in designer suits, knew the correct wines to order with dinner and had recently introduced her to Cabernet Sauvignon. Judging from the leather-bound volumes lining his bookshelves, he was very well read. The perfect Renaissance man come to life, she decided.

As if conjured up by her thoughts, Peter stuck his head through the doorway at that moment and smiled apologetically. "I'll just be a few more minutes. I've got one more call to make, and then I'll order dinner."

She smiled effortlessly, which surprised her, considering she'd not had much to smile about before meeting the handsome attorney. But she felt totally at ease with him. She trusted him. "Take your time. I had a late lunch with Meredith."

"How is she? Did she seem…upset about anything?"

Sally shook her head, her curiosity piqued. "No. Should she be?"

"Just wondering." Flashing her a grin to conceal his relief, Peter cursed inwardly for worrying about Adam. The man could handle himself. Hell, he ran everyone's life with perfect aplomb. "Be right back."

Gazing at her reflection in the antique mirror hanging by the door, Sally was pleased with her appearance this evening. She'd chosen the black knit dress carefully, had taken extra pains with her hair and had applied her makeup as Meredith had instructed, with subtle shades and a light hand. But though she looked presentable, she still couldn't understand why a polished, successful attorney like Peter Webber, who could have his pick of women, had chosen to bestow his attentions on her.

Though Sally had finished high school, her education had never gone beyond, and she didn't consider herself to be a scintillating conversationalist, though she was a damn sight smarter than some of those women Meredith had been interviewing as bridal candidates.

She and Peter did seem to have a lot in common, anyway—their love of old Western movies, for one thing, and sadly, the tragic deaths of their parents. They had no trouble communicating, and for that she was grateful. Peter Webber was the first man she'd met in a very long time with whom she felt a strong connection.

Professional counseling had revealed that her unhealthy relationship with her ex-fiancé, Dwayne—the last in a string of unhealthy relationships—had been based on her need to be taken care of, her unrealistic expectations about love.

On her own since the age of seventeen when her parents had been killed in a freak boating accident, Sally hadn't been able to adjust to life on her own. She'd been thrust out into the cruel world to fend for herself, and it had been easier to find someone who would take care of her, to keep her loneliness at bay, even if that meant abasing herself to the abusive ones she had the unfortunate knack of always finding.

She'd learned since that the only person she could truly rely on was herself, that being alone did not necessarily have to mean being lonely, that aloneness had benefits, like quiet solitude for reading, or learning how to type and operate a computer, which in turn had opened up a whole new world to her.

Sally was proud of the small steps she'd taken toward independence, which was just one of many reasons she didn't want to foster an intimate relationship with Peter, grow dependent on him, though she desired him more than she'd ever thought herself capable of desiring anyone.

"I bet you're starved."

Peter's voice jolted her out of her reverie, and she smiled softly at him. She was starved. But she wasn't quite ready to feast. She only hoped Peter would still be on the menu when she regained her appetite.

Chapter Thirteen

"Adam! Adam Morgan, where are you? When I get my hands on you—" Meredith slid to a halt at the sight of the three men standing in Adam's study, her face flushing red. One she knew—the one she was going to kill. But the other two men were strangers, and she was horribly embarrassed to have been caught behaving in such an unprofessional manner. If they were part of the wedding party, she would have to resign as consultant. Even she had her humiliation limits.

"Come in, Meredith. I've been expecting you." Adam motioned her forward, smiling softly and looking not the least bit surprised by her harried arrival. "My guess is that you've been to see your mother."

The reminder of why she'd come had her green eyes flashing angrily, and she stomped in. "Excuse me," she said to the strangers, "but I need to talk to Mr. Morgan for a minute." Tugging on Adam's sleeve, she dragged him out into the hallway where she could speak to him privately, ignoring the raised eyebrows of the two distinguished-looking men.

"How could you, Adam? My mother is very sick, and you had no right to go to the nursing home to enlist her in this ridiculous quest of yours to marry me. I absolutely forbid you to—''

He held up his hand to silence her. ''I'm sorry about your mother, Meredith. I had no idea she was so ill and that she bore me such animosity, or I'd never have mentioned my plan to marry you.''

Noting the sincerity in his eyes, the contriteness in his voice, she inclined her head, her anger deflating slowly. ''Mom was beside herself when I arrived at the home, Adam. I had to have her sedated and couldn't leave there until early this morning.''

Clasping her hand, he squeezed it gently, then brought it to his lips for a kiss. ''I'm truly sorry. But my visit was not entirely in vain.''

''Adam—'' The warning in her voice was unmistakable.

''Hear me out, before you chew off the rest of my hide. Okay?''

She agreed to listen, and he led her to a small high-backed settee that looked as if it had been used during the Spanish Inquisition, it was that uncomfortable.

''Those men in my office are heart specialists. I've brought them here to consult on your mother's condition.''

Her forehead wrinkled in confusion. ''Heart specialists? I don't understand.''

''I'll explain everything to you afterward, but for now their time is limited and I'd like you to talk to them before they have to leave. They can explain far better than I what I have in mind. Will you do that?''

She finally relented, though her expression was filled with exasperation. ''Do I have a choice? I get the feeling you'd have me straightjacketed and committed to an asylum if I refuse.''

"Maybe just confined to bed," he said with a devilish wink, and she blushed to the roots of her hair.

"Dr. Robertson and Dr. Cushman are from the Johns Hopkins University Medical Center in Baltimore," he explained. "They're the foremost experts in the field of heart transplantation."

"But—''

He pressed his fingers to her lips. "Later."

After being escorted into the study, she forced a small smile for the two men while Adam performed the introduction.

"Miss Baxter, Mr. Morgan has put us in touch with your mother's physician, Dr. Carpenter, whom we have consulted at length about her condition," Dr. Cushman informed her. A tall man with white hair and kind blue eyes, he boasted a tanned complexion that bespoke his passion for tennis and other outdoor sports.

"We were allowed to give your mother a rather extensive examination, study her history and medical tests, all with Dr. Carpenter's permission and assistance, of course," Dr. Robertson added. He wasn't nearly as tall or distinguished as Dr. Cushman, but his eyes held the same amount of compassion. Judging from the thickness of his lenses, not to mention his waist, Meredith concluded that Dr. Robertson spent most of his time in front of a computer module rather than on the tennis court or golf course.

"We're confident your mother's life can be saved with a transplant," he continued. "We're willing to accept her into the transplant program at Johns Hopkins, register her name with UNOS—The United

Network for Organ Sharing—and perform the necessary operation when a proper matched organ becomes available, provided you can obtain her permission.

"Mrs. Baxter seems resigned to her fate, if you don't mind my saying so."

Meredith took a moment to digest everything. Adam had gone to a great deal of trouble to bring these noted physicians to Morgantown. She'd read about Dr. Cushman's success with heart transplantation, but never imagined that she would actually meet him face-to-face, let alone discuss the possibility of his operating on her mother. The entire episode was too surreal for her to comprehend.

Finally she said, "My mother is resigned to her fate, doctor. We've known for a while that a transplant could possibly save her life, but until now have never had that confirmed.

"Unfortunately neither my mother nor I have the resources to pay for such an operation, let alone the expenses we would incur during her convalescence." She'd been told by her mother's insurance company that the cost for such an operation could exceed one million dollars, and that they would only cover a very small portion. "I appreciate your coming, but—"

Stepping forward, Dr. Cushman reached for her hand. It was warm and comforting, and she decided that even Marcus Welby could have taken lessons in bedside manner from the older man. "We understand about financial considerations, Miss Baxter, which is why I think you should speak to Mr. Morgan before making any decision.

"It's necessary for Dr. Robertson and me to return to Baltimore within the hour, but we can make the necessary arrangements in a matter of hours to have your mother transported to Johns Hopkins once you give the word.''

Meredith stared transfixed at the doorway for several moments after the doctors departed. Her fondest hope—to save her mother's life—had just been laid before her.

But at what cost? And she wasn't thinking about money.

''I won't marry you, Adam, even if you pay for a heart transplant,'' she told him flat-out, ignoring his startled, somewhat wounded expression. ''So if that's your motive in doing this—''

''Dammit, Meredith, but you make it hard for a man to right an old wrong.''

''And you make it hard for a woman not to believe you don't have ulterior motives. After all, you've gone to some rather unusual lengths to convince me to marry you.''

''That's true, but this situation doesn't have anything to do with the other.'' He turned toward the credenza behind him. ''Would you care for a glass of wine?''

''All right.'' It was a little early in the day, but what the heck? Maybe alcohol would render everything crystal clear. Adam certainly hadn't as yet.

Seating herself in one of the wing chairs flanking the fireplace, she took the glass he offered, waiting impatiently while he seated himself in the other. ''It's 'later,''' she reminded him, needing answers to her many questions.

Adam was uncertain how Meredith would react to his taking control of such a delicate situation. She already thought him too presumptuous, but he decided to take his chances, anyway. The surgery would benefit not only Louise Baxter, it would also lighten the burden on Meredith's shoulders. It couldn't have been easy for her having her mother's life placed in her hands and not being able to do a thing to save it.

"Your mother apprised me of the circumstances surrounding your father's death. It seems she holds Morgan Coal Mining and Manufacturing responsible for events leading up to and succeeding Henry Baxter's demise."

Oh, Mother! What have you done?

"And after a bit of investigation I have to agree that we were partly to blame."

His admission moved her, as did his willingness to accept responsibility for something that happened a long time ago, something he had nothing to do with, something that in reality was no one's fault but the Almighty's. And Meredith wasn't about to cast blame in His direction.

Reaching out, she touched his hand. "Nonsense. You're not to blame. My mother is bitter because her life didn't turn out the way she'd planned. She misses my dad, hates being ill, and it's colored the way she looks at things."

"Nonetheless, I feel we owe her." He explained at length what his investigation had uncovered thus far, then added, "I'm sorry, Meredith, for what you and your mother had to endure because of our oversight. My company should have been there for you. It's never been our policy to treat employees callously, as your father was apparently treated.

"Morgan Coal Mining and Manufacturing is a company with a heart, and we'd like to give that heart to your mother. It won't make up for your father's death, but—''

''Adam! I... I don't know what to say.''

''Please say you'll accept my apology and forgive my father for his lack of action in this matter all those years ago. Allistair Morgan was a hard man, uncaring at times to his own family, but he always held the highest regard and admiration for the people who worked for him, and I'm sure that included your father.''

''I do,'' she said softly, her eyes filling with tears. ''And I thank you for wanting to make things right. But that doesn't mean I hold you responsible for my mother's heart condition or my father's death, Adam. I certainly don't expect you to pay for a heart transplant, though it is the nicest thing anyone's ever offered to do for me. I apologize for having suspected you of having an ulterior motive. I was wrong.''

''As much as I'd like to marry you, Meredith, I would never hold your mother's failing health over your head. I hope you give me more credit than that. Besides,'' he added, grinning, ''I'm not giving up on the idea of marrying you. I just have to find another way to convince you.''

Deciding in that instant that Adam Morgan's heart was worth another shot, Meredith set down her wine, crossed the small distance between them, then plopped herself onto his lap, circling his neck with her arms, much to his surprise and, judging from the rock-hard response of his body, delight.

He might not realize yet that he loved her, but no man went to as much trouble for a woman as Adam had gone for her and not possess some feelings. It gave her hope.

"Why don't you kiss me for starters. It always gets me in the mood for other things." Her smile was deliciously naughty, her eyes twinkling at his shocked expression.

"Other things?"

She loosened his tie and began to unbutton his shirt. "I suggest you lock the door, Mr. Morgan, or Mrs. Fishburn's going to get an eyeful."

He jumped to his feet, carting her to the door with him. "You constantly surprise me, Meredith."

"And you, Mr. Morgan, are without a doubt the most exasperating," she kissed his chin, "the most difficult man—" she moved her lips to his mouth "—I have ever encountered."

"Thank you," he said, sweeping his tongue over her teeth before lowering her onto the sofa. "That's music to my ears."

"You're impossible." She trailed her tongue down his bare chest.

"Mmm," he conceded, then bared her breasts and lapped at her nipples.

"Arrogant." Her hand moved to cup him and she squeezed gently.

"Meredith!"

"And very…very…hard…very hardheaded indeed, Mr. Morgan." She tugged down his zipper, releasing the pulsing member and clasping it in her hand.

"Two can play at this game, Miss Baxter." Beads of sweat formed on his upper lip as Adam reached under her skirt to find another surprise—thigh-high stockings, which were no impediment to his destination. Tearing off the wisp of material covering her, he palmed her with slow, circular motions until she grew wet.

"Adam!" Her groan of pleasure filled the room.

Unable to wait any longer, he entered her quickly, plunging into the depths of her core, their mating fast, frenzied and fulfilling. When they had both felt satiated and floated back down to earth, Adam kissed her softly on the lips and sighed the sigh of a man totally contented with the world and everything in it.

"You're very special to me, love. I hope you realize that."

Her dreamy smile was one of pure satisfaction. "I'm beginning to suspect."

Suddenly the grandfather clock chimed two, and her eyes, which had been closed, flew wide open. "I nearly forgot." Pushing at his chest, she sat up, "I've got an appointment in thirty minutes," then began a frantic search for her underwear.

With a somewhat guilty expression, Adam brought forth her panties—what remained of them, anyway—dangling the wispy scrap of black lace from his forefinger. "I guess I got a little carried away in the heat of the moment. You'll have to go without these."

Her face flamed as she stared at the torn remnants of what used to be Victoria's Secret's bargain of the month. Her skirt was quite short, and she was likely to pull a Sharon Stone if she met the Weavers without anything beneath it.

"I'd offer you a pair of mine, but I don't think they'd fit."

The smile she shot him took away not only his self-satisfied smirk, but his breath, forcing him to lean back against the sofa. "I hope you spend the remainder of the day thinking about me without a stitch of clothing on beneath this suit." A black lace bra, which matched the underpants, landed squarely on his head. He took it in his hands, staring wide-eyed at it, then at her. "Have a nice day, Adam," she said before departing.

HE WATCHED HER LEAVE. Damn, but she was a fine-looking woman, Curtis thought. She wore no bra, he could tell. And he wanted nothing more than to have his fill of her.

And he would. Soon.

Now that he'd thought out a plan, there was no way he was going to leave Meredith Baxter out of it.

Soon, he thought. Very soon.

THE HAIRS ON THE BACK of Meredith's neck prickled, and she paused by the car door, key in hand, squinting against the sun at the woods across the road from Adam's house. She saw nothing but green-leafed trees, thick underbrush and birds flitting from branch to branch, but she still had the distinct feeling someone was watching her.

For days she'd had the uneasy feeling of being watched. Even at home behind locked doors and drawn drapes she felt as if eyes were upon her. It was silly, she knew, and obviously stress related. She'd been working hard on a number of weddings, and her mother's deteriorating health, combined with Adam's unrelenting pursuit, had taken its toll.

Turning back toward the mansion, she saw Adam standing at the window and breathed a sigh of relief. She returned his wave, chiding herself for her over-active imagination. Then, checking her watch, she muttered a colorful epithet under her breath and plunged into the driver's seat, forgetting her imagined fears for the reality of meeting her persnickety client, Fran Weaver, without any underpants on.

And if that wasn't scary enough, the subsequent meeting she would have with her mother this afternoon. The meeting that could save Louise Baxter's life, if she could convince the stubborn woman to have the transplant operation.

PAUSING OUTSIDE her mother's room, Meredith crossed herself, even though she wasn't Catholic, said a brief prayer that Louise would be reasonable for a change and entered, forcing a huge smile to her face.

Smiles could hide lies very effectively, and her mother could always detect when Meredith was lying. Today she intended to tell a whopper.

"Hi, Mom! How are you feeling? Better I hope."

Louise's eyes widened in surprise. "What are you doing here so early? I wasn't expecting you till later."

Reaching behind her back, she brought forth a bag with the colonel's cheery face on it, and her mother licked her lips. "I've brought some illicit fried chicken for us to share. I've got some good news, and I thought we should celebrate." There was nothing her mother liked more than fried chicken, and Meredith wasn't above using a bit of bribery to soften her up.

"Lock the door," Louise cautioned, casting a nervous glance in its direction. "If Nurse Mullins comes in and sees what we're eating, she'll put me on a diet of beef bouillon for weeks."

They settled themselves at the small maple table like a couple of treasure-laden pirates, and Meredith served up the bounty, pushing a paper plate toward her mother. "You mentioned good news," Louise said between bites, unable to hide the pleasure on her face at eating something so wickedly unhealthy for her.

Meredith began her fabrication. Soon her mother would be able to eat all the fried chicken she wanted, and Meredith knew the lies would be worthwhile. "Adam Morgan's secretary contacted me today. Apparently she found an old insurance policy on Dad while cleaning out some files."

"An insurance policy? But I thought we'd received all of his benefits after his death."

"So did I, but apparently we were wrong. The documents are old but still in force. It seems Dad left you a tidy sum of money."

Louise's eyes widened, and she set down her forkful of coleslaw. "How tidy?"

Meredith grinned. "Enough to pay for a heart transplant."

"But, but— That's an awful lot of money, Merry." The shocked woman's face whitened more than usual, her hand flying to her chest to cover her rapidly beating heart. Meredith knew a moment of concern, but then her mother's color returned.

Reaching out across the table, Meredith clasped her mother's hand. "It's what we've been praying for, Mom. Your chance to get well, be normal again, kick the dust of this place off your shoes."

Tears filled the woman's eyes. "I hardly know what to say, what to think. An insurance policy." She shook her head. "It's unbelievable."

"Aren't you the one who's always telling me that God works in mysterious ways?" God and Adam Morgan, Meredith thought. An intriguing combination if ever there was one.

"I may live to see you married yet, Merry."

Kissing her mother's cheek, she replied, "It's okay to be optimistic, Mom, but let's not get carried away about the marriage thing, okay? I've got more important things to worry about, like getting you well."

Louise's chin, dripping with chicken grease, jutted out mutinously. "I intend to watch you walk down the aisle on the arm of your husband. I also plan to be in the hospital waiting room when you give birth to my first grandchild."

Swallowing with some difficulty, Meredith forced a small smile, thinking that after what had occurred between her and Adam this afternoon, her mother could very well get her wish.

In the heat of the moment, she and Adam had gone sleeveless once again.

Chapter Fourteen

While Louise waited anxiously in the Baltimore hospital for an organ match to be found, Meredith did the same at home, filling her time with work, studying the latest information on heart transplantation and spending time with Adam.

The two had been nearly inseparable since her mother's departure a week ago, and Meredith felt guilty at being so deliriously happy during the woman's difficult ordeal.

To assuage that guilt she called Louise three times a day, without fail, to check on how she was handling things and to offer reassurance. Her mother had put on a brave face, but Meredith knew she was terrified. She planned to visit her during the upcoming long Memorial weekend, and, using the statistics she'd gleaned from her research, hoped to allay some of her fears. Adam and the kids intended to accompany her, which would make everything perfect.

If only an organ could be located.

Adam touched the end of Meredith's nose with the tip of his finger, then pulled her into his arms, hugging her tightly to his chest. "Will you stop frowning and kiss me? I can't stand to see you so upset." If making love could keep her mind off her mother's condition, then he felt obligated to provide the distraction. He'd never made love to any woman and felt the way he did now—all warm and contented and happier than he'd been in his entire life.

Was that love? Was he in love with Meredith? If only he knew for sure. He'd even read a few of those romance novels she was so crazy about, to see if they could provide him with the answer. He'd enjoyed them, though he had no intention of admitting that to anyone, but he was still as confused as ever about his feelings for her.

One thing he wasn't confused about was his unrelenting desire for her. It was a hunger he couldn't satisfy, a burning within him that even the coldest shower couldn't quell. "Make love with me again. I can't get my fill of you."

Caressing his cheek, she kissed him softly on the lips. "I can't seem to get enough of you, either, Adam. It's scary how much I want you. But I'm going to be too worn out to visit my mother if we keep this up. I might not be able to walk."

She'd been barely awake when Adam had shown up at her door at seven o'clock that morning, holding a bag of mouth-watering croissants and two large cups of gourmet coffee. Smoldering looks had been exchanged over the hurried meal, then they'd found their way to her bed by seven-fifteen and had been there ever since.

Grinning, he reached for her breast and began fondling her nipple. His touch elicited a moan. "You won't have to," he informed her. "We're taking a private jet."

That moan turned quickly to openmouthed wonder, and she stared at him as if he'd lost his mind. "I have a perfectly good car, Adam, and it won't take long to drive to Baltimore. A few hours at most. I won't have you spending money needlessly. You've done enough already."

She intended to keep track of every penny he spent. Someday—maybe when she won the lottery—she'd pay him back. She'd never purposely used another human being for her own ends before, and she wasn't going to start with Adam, no matter how much money he had or how much he insisted—make that *demanded*—she take it. Aside from the fact that she loved him too much, that sort of behavior just grated against her upbringing, falling into the "never a borrower or a lender be" category.

Stretching long legs out in front of him, Adam's toes hit the footboard of the bed. He frowned. Double beds were just too darn small for his large frame. "Remind me to buy you a new bed. If we're going to make love at your house, then I need a larger—"

She knew him too well, and her brow lifted. "Don't change the subject. I said, we're driving."

Still toying with her breast, as if it was the most fascinating object he'd ever discovered, he ignored her tortured gasps of pleasure and replied, "The kids have been begging for an airplane ride. I thought next weekend would be the perfect time to let them have their fun." In less than a month Megan and Andrew would be back in court for the final round of custody proceedings. They might as well enjoy themselves now, in the event—

No! He refused to think in any terms other than the fact that he would marry Meredith and adopt his niece and nephew. He hadn't wanted to pressure her while her mother was in the hospital, but time was quickly slipping away, as were his chances with the court.

The thought depressed him, so he turned his attention to more uplifting matters. "You've got beautiful breasts, love."

Lowering his head, he tongued her nipple with agonizing thoroughness, and streaks of white-hot desire shot through her, heating her blood to the hard-boiled stage. "You're not playing fair, Adam," she protested, her voice breathless with desire. "First you use the kids to soften me up, and now you're intent on seducing me again. You're just not playing fair."

"All's fair in love, war and business."

He trailed his tongue down her chest to land in her navel. "Mmmm. You've got the most delectable belly button. I could spend the rest of my life nestled right here."

But he didn't.

Soon he moved lower to place scorching kisses on the inside of her thighs. "Ooooh! Stop that! You're— *Oooh!*"

"You smell like peaches and cream. Do you taste as good, I wonder?"

It was the scented body wash, but she didn't bother to answer the rhetorical question, because Adam's tongue had slipped lower and was doing a taste test of its own.

"Adam." His name slipped out on a sigh.

Gripping the sheets, as if they could keep her anchored to the bed, she felt herself floating higher and higher with every flick of his delectably clever tongue. "I...I can't take any more. All right," she conceded with a tortured gasp. "We'll go by plane."

She heard him chuckle softly. That was the last thing she heard, because her head filled with a peculiar ringing noise, and her body took off of its own accord to land somewhere in the vicinity of the ceiling fan.

If the *Guinness Book of Records* had had a category for most powerful lovemaking, the one she'd just experienced would have been at the top of the list. "Wow!" she exclaimed when her breathing had finally returned to normal, not realizing she'd spoken aloud until she heard Adam's amused laughter again.

"You'd better answer the phone. It's ringing off the hook," he told her.

"The phone?" She shook her head to clear it, then realized what he was talking about. "The phone's ringing."

He handed her the portable from the nightstand. "I believe I already said that."

Her look was filled with annoyance, his with amusement.

"Miss Baxter, this is Dr. Cushman."

Meredith's heart, which was already churning like a cement mixer, slammed against her ribs. If something had happened to her mother— "Is everything all right? Is my mom okay?" She held her breath and didn't release it until he replied.

"She's fine, Miss Baxter. In fact, your mother's going to be even better in a very short time. We've found an organ. We've scheduled the transplant operation for first thing tomorrow morning. Can you be here?"

"They found a match!" she told Adam excitedly, her eyes filling with tears. And to the doctor, she said, "Yes. Yes, I can." In a daze she handed the phone back to the man who had made it all possible, wondering if she could love him any more than she already did.

She decided she could.

Adam kissed her cheek, relieved at the joy registered on her face, reflected in her voice, in the brilliance of her eyes bright with tears. "I'm happy for you, love."

"My mother's going to live. She's going to be all right. I just know it."

Aware of the problems associated with heart transplants, because he'd been doing some research of his own, he advised caution. He didn't want Meredith to get her hopes up only to have them dashed. She might not recover from such a disappointment, and the blame would be his to bear.

"Let's take this one step at a time. You know the procedure isn't one hundred percent foolproof." Heart transplants did have an eighty percent, one-year survival rate, which was very encouraging, despite the possibility of organ rejection, infection and numerous other variables that had to be taken into account.

Not listening to a word he'd said, Meredith threw her arms around his neck and kissed him—not passionately, but with gratitude, love and hope that she could win this wonderful man's heart. "Thank you for doing this, Adam. I don't know how I can ever repay you."

He stroked her hair, dried her tears with his lips and groaned when his body responded to the feel of hers pressed against him. It was on the tip of his tongue to say, "Then marry me," but he didn't. He couldn't bring himself to put his needs before hers. He cared too damn much.

"I'm sure we'll think of something, love."

"ARE YOU SURE I can handle things while you're out, Randall? I'm nervous about being left alone in the store. What if I do something wrong? What if that nasty Mrs. O'Connor decides to stop in to pick up her mother-of-the-groom dress? She's so snooty. I always feel like poor white trash around her."

Randall flashed the worried woman an empathetic look, knowing exactly how she felt. "Joan O'Connor isn't one of my favorite people, either, Sally, but she's a good-paying customer, and we can't afford to alienate her. She's got lots of rich friends who are every bit as annoying as she is, and who are likely to shop here on her recommendation.

"Trust me. I've had my share of the woman's pointed looks and sly remarks. Just ignore her if she happens to come in. She's obviously very unhappy, even with all her money and supposed standing in the community."

Then to lighten the moment, he picked up a piece of silk fabric off the chair, draped it around his shoulders like a fur stole and mimicked in a falsetto voice, "My dear, dear girl, don't you know who I am? The O'Connors have lived in Morgantown since before coal was invented." He rolled his big blue eyes, and Sally burst out laughing, taking the fabric he handed her.

"I won't be able to keep a straight face now, if she does come in. Thanks."

"I'll only be gone a couple of hours. I've got to run over to the school and pick up a few things. If you get stuck, give me a call on my cellular.'' He held the palm-size phone up for her inspection. ''Isn't this just the cutest thing you've ever seen?'' he asked, clipping it to his belt. ''And so *très chic*.''

Sally nodded absently. Randall liked waxing poetic over his newly acquired purchases, whether that be telephones, underwear or flavored coffees, and she'd gotten used to tuning him out. Meredith had advised when she'd hired her that tuning Randall out was the only way she'd be able to keep her sanity while working with him. As lovable and considerate as the man was, and as much as she and Meredith adored him, he did have his moments.

''All right,'' she finally said. ''But don't blame me if Meredith fires both of us when she gets back from Baltimore.''

''Meredith has her hands full right now. The last thing she's going to be thinking of is this place. Did you see her rapt expression when she told us about the private jet? She was so euphoric she could have flown to Baltimore on her own power.''

''Mr. Morgan's been very kind.''

''He loves her. He's just too stupid to realize it yet.'' He let loose with a deeply dramatic sigh. ''Armani suits and Hermes ties are wasted on a man like that.''

Sally wondered why Randall always reduced everything to clothing. It made her wonder what he thought of her own pitiful designerless wardrobe. ''You'd think when two people are in love, as Meredith and Adam Morgan obviously are, things would go a little more smoothly for them,'' she said.

''I happen to know two other people who are in love, and who aren't doing a darn thing about it,'' he remarked, noting the flush rising to her cheeks now that she'd finally figured out who he was talking about.

Randall was having one of his moments, Sally concluded, trying to keep her temper in check. "I'm not ready. And you don't know if Peter's in love with me. We haven't known each other that long." But oh, it was a magnificent notion. The attorney was everything she wanted in a man—kind, caring, great with children. Not to mention sexy as all get-out.

"Don't I? The man practically drools every time he comes in here. If you don't put him out of his misery soon, I may have to take the poor guy out back and shoot him."

Sally's gasp filled the room, making the law student grin. "Randall Cosby, what a terrible thing to say!"

"Give the guy a break, Sally. Kiss him, make love to him, then marry him. Peter's a good guy. And his threads are top-notch. You can always judge a man by his clothes."

Sally was tempted to say something to that last comment—Dwayne had been a clothes horse—but Randall was already out the door before she had the chance.

She shook her head at the absurdity of the man's comments, no matter how well-intentioned. Marry Peter? How perfectly ridiculous. As if he would actually want to marry someone like her. Someone with such a sordid past.

Putting Randall's unsettling comments out of her mind, she began straightening up the reception room. Fortunately mornings were usually quiet at the store, and the fact that it was raining would keep business to a minimum until Randall got back. At least that's what Sally hoped.

She was on her hands and knees, picking up an armful of bridal magazines that some thoughtless customer had dumped on the floor when the door opened.

"That's what I like to see, a woman on her knees. It gives a man such a rush."

She stood quickly, not recognizing the voice or the man who'd stepped into the store, and her face filled with color at what his words implied. Filled with instant dislike, she forced herself to be polite, remembering that he was a customer. "May I help you?" she asked in a businesslike voice.

Brushing droplets of water from his hair, he wiped his hands on his pantlegs. "I'm here to see Meredith Baxter. Is she here?"

"No," she replied, wondering how much to reveal. "I'm sorry, but Miss Baxter is out of town on a personal matter. I'm not sure when she'll be returning. If you had an appointment with her, then perhaps I can help." Meredith hadn't mentioned any customer appointments, but she may have just forgotten in all the confusion and rush to get to the hospital.

Curtis Tremayne cursed inwardly his bad luck. He'd finally intended to put his plan into action and had taken quite a risk in coming into town today. But he'd deemed the act a necessity. And now this.

Unwilling to give his hand away, he smiled smoothly, and like the chameleon he'd learned to be over the years, changed his manner, knowing how a little charm could soothe even the most skittish of women, as this one appeared to be. She'd been wringing her hands, though he doubted she knew it. He, however, made it a point to observe everything.

"And who might you be?" he asked.

"Sally. Sally Jacobs, Miss Baxter's assistant." She was actually Randall's assistant, but that took too long to explain. And it wasn't any of this man's business, anyway. "May I give Miss Baxter a message? Have her call you when she returns?"

The man smiled, somewhat sinisterly, she thought, but Sally couldn't help but notice how handsome he was, despite the facial hair—she hated beards— though his appearance was rather shabby, as though he'd fallen on hard times recently. He smelled of cigarette smoke and that horrible deodorizer that was found in public restrooms.

"No. No message. I'll catch up with her another time."

"If you're sure?"

"I've never been more sure about anything," he said before disappearing out the door.

The stranger's odd comment coupled with the irritated way he'd said it made the hair on the back of Sally's neck prickle. Some sixth sense told her that the man wasn't all he pretended to be. She'd met enough bastards in her lifetime to recognize one when she saw one.

Heading toward the telephone, Sally was about to call Randall when Peter walked in.

Flooded with relief, she rushed forward, practically throwing herself into his arms. "Peter! I'm so glad to see you."

Peter smiled a bit uncertainly at her reaction. Sally wasn't usually this demonstrative. Then he noticed how tightly she was gripping his sleeve, how her eyes were filled with something akin to fear, and he wondered what had put it there.

"I'm happy to see you, too. But you look upset. What's wrong?" If that ex-fiancé of hers had put in an appearance, he wanted to know about it. Peter intended to make certain the scumbag never laid hands on Sally again. The woman was his. He loved her. And he would do everything in his power to protect her.

Her breathing was still a bit ragged when she said, "I'm sorry I overreacted. You know how I am." She smiled apologetically, then asked, "Did you happen to see that man who just left here? The one who looked rather unkempt?

He shook his head. "No. I had my head buried in my briefcase for a few moments, then Adam called to let me know they'd arrived safely in Baltimore, and I spent the next few minutes talking to him on the phone. Why? Was he bothering you?"

"I— There was just something peculiar about him. He asked for Meredith, and when I told him she wasn't here, he seemed almost angered by my response. I probably imagined it, but—"

The attorney grew immediately suspicious. "What did he look like? Would you recognize him again if you saw him?"

"Probably. He was quite nice looking actually, even with his beard. But I couldn't help feeling that he was up to something. I guess after all I've been through I tend to get suspicious of people. It's a flaw I'm trying to correct."

A sick feeling of dread formed in the pit of Peter's stomach at the fact that Sally's stranger might not be a stranger at all. "I'll be right back."

He hurried out to his car and returned in a matter of moments with his briefcase, which he set on the counter. Retrieving an official-looking document, he handed it to her. "Is this the man who came into the store today?"

She gasped, noting the name at the bottom. "That's him. Even with his beard I recognize him. I could never forget those eyes. They were so cold, so remote." She shivered. "Curtis Tremayne. Meredith told me about what he did. But why would he come here looking for Meredith? Why would he risk getting caught? That doesn't make any sense."

Peter wondered the same thing, not liking any of the possibilities he came up with. And not liking the fact that he had frightened Sally. It was obvious Tremayne was up to something and that something involved Meredith. But what? And why? He didn't even know her.

But Adam did. And Peter knew Tremayne hated Adam.

"I've got to notify the police about this right away." And he had to let Adam know that Meredith might be in danger.

Refocusing his attention on Sally, he gave her a reassuring smile. "You're safe now. I wouldn't let anything happen to you, you know that, don't you?" She nodded, and he gave her shoulder a squeeze. "I want you to call me right away if Tremayne should happen to come back. I don't think he will," he added quickly when her eyes widened. "He has no reason to, now that he knows Meredith isn't here."

She swallowed the huge lump of fear in her throat, worried for Meredith's safety more than her own. "Are you sure you have to leave?"

The apprehension on her face gave him pause, but he had to get the ball rolling. If the police responded quickly, Tremayne could be caught. "Call Randall and tell him what's happened, okay? Tell him to come back to the store?"

"I will. But— Well— Will I see you again?" It was bold of her to ask, but she missed him so much when he wasn't with her.

Kiss him, Randall had said. *Make love to him. Marry him.* Well she had no control over the latter, but there was certainly something she could do about the other.

"How about dinner tonight?" he asked. "We could go to The Glass House Grill, as we'd previously planned."

"I have a better idea," she said, fingering the button on his suit jacket. "Why don't you come over to my apartment tonight and I'll cook you dinner. I'm actually a very good cook."

Her lips were so inviting, so delectable, that Peter had to forcibly restrain himself from hauling her into his arms and kissing her. He knew if he forced the issue, she'd retreat, as she had all the other times they'd been together. "I'll bring the wine," he offered.

"Peter."

Her tempting smile and big brown eyes were more than he could handle. Tossing aside caution and most of his better judgment, he wrapped his arms about her, nuzzling her neck and ear, working his way to her mouth, then he paused. "You're torturing me, Sally. I can't wait to kiss you any longer."

"Then don't," she replied, pressing her lips against his, and allowing herself to feel once again.

It was time. Peter was the right man, she was sure of it. And one other thing she was sure of, if her heart could be believed: she loved him.

Chapter Fifteen

"Uncle *Addaamm!*" Megan shot her uncle a pleading look, her small face scrunched with frustration. "You're getting those stupid seeds all over the pages of my coloring book."

"It's ugly, anyway," Andrew pointed out before returning his attention to his own book on dinosaurs. Megan stuck out her tongue, wiggling it back and forth like a lizard.

"Sorry," Adam said, then gazed at Meredith who was asleep in the seat across from him to make certain she hadn't been disturbed by the kids' bickering. Sleeping the sleep of the dead, she had not awakened, and he was relieved.

They'd just spent an emotionally draining few days in Baltimore. Now on their way back to Morgantown in the private jet he'd hired, Meredith was both physically and mentally exhausted after spending the last few days at her mother's bedside, maintaining constant vigil in case a complication resulting from the transplant should occur.

He'd done his best to entertain the kids during that time by taking them to the aquarium and an Orioles game at Camden Yards, but the tension surrounding

Louise Baxter's operation had sapped all of their strength and shortened tempers considerably.

Meredith's mother had survived the operation. Both Dr. Cushman and Dr. Robertson had given the thumbs-up sign when emerging from the operating room, which had given them hope that Mrs. Baxter was going to make it. Her prognosis for a full recovery was good, though it would take a while before they knew for sure that the transplanted heart wouldn't be rejected, and she'd be remaining in Baltimore for the time being.

She was a tough lady, and so was her daughter.

Adam was glad he'd been there for Meredith during the emotional ordeal. She'd held up well, considering how frightened she'd been, though there'd been times when the tension had gotten to her and she'd broken down and cried. He'd held her close during those times, whispering words of comfort, offering his strength to bolster hers.

Being with her at such a time had made him feel as if they were two halves coming together to make a whole. And he realized he liked the feeling.

"When's Meredith gonna wake up? I want her to read me a story."

"She's sleeping 'cause her mom's sick. Don't you know nothing?" Andrew shook his head, clearly irritated that his younger sister could be so totally dense.

Noting the hurt look on his niece's face, Adam held out his arms, and she crawled up onto his lap. He treasured the closeness that had developed between the kids and him, and he had Meredith to thank for it. Without her encouragement and support, her gentle insistence that he take the first step toward furthering their relationship, he would never have opened up to them, felt comfortable around them.

"Is Mrs. Baxter going to get all well, Uncle Adam? Meredith said her bear, Morgan, was the first thing she packed to take with her to the hospital." The little girl had been inordinately pleased by the news.

Adam's brow shot up. "Mrs. Baxter has a teddy bear named Morgan?" How very peculiar, considering the woman's distaste for him.

The child explained about the bear, then asked, "You sure do like Meredith, don't you, Uncle Adam?"

"Well o'course he likes her, dummy. Why do you think he kisses her all the time? Have you given her a baby yet, Uncle Adam?" Andrew's question made his uncle's face turn crimson and Megan's eyes widen at the possibility.

"A baby! We're gonna gets us a baby?" She began to bounce up and down.

"No." Adam gritted his teeth, holding her in place with as much firmness as his voice held at the moment. "And, Andrew, I'd like to remind you to mind your own business and keep your voice down. Children should be seen and not heard." That was one of his mother's favorite sayings, and Adam had to agree that it held a great deal of merit, especially as it pertained to an eight-year-old boy with a mouth as wide as a mine shaft.

Her eyes still closed, Meredith smiled inwardly as she eavesdropped on their conversation. It seemed Andrew and his uncle had already had a discussion about babies and her possible involvement with them. Adam must have been totally mortified. She could just picture him stammering and hemming and hawing, and wished she'd been a fly on the wall at that discussion.

Her hand resting on her abdomen, she wondered what it would be like to carry Adam's child beneath her breast. It would be a boy, she was certain, with dark hair, silver eyes and an engaging smile that was sure to melt the hearts of females everywhere.

They hadn't used protection on several of the occasions they'd come together, and it was entirely possible that the fantasy could become a reality, though she'd seen no signs of it yet. Of course, her periods had always been irregular, so there was no way of knowing for sure, short of taking one of those home pregnancy tests.

Did she dare?

What if she found out she was pregnant? Then what?

Oh, Adam would surely marry her. He wanted to, anyway, to suit his own purposes, and he wasn't the type to abandon his own flesh and blood, at any rate.

But what kind of a marriage would it be?

Did she have enough love for both of them?

Tired of questions she had no answers to, she opened her eyes and smiled at the millionaire's bloodred face, feigning innocence. "Why, Adam, what's wrong? Are you ill? You look like you're burning up." She leaned forward and placed her palm on his forehead, knowing full well what she'd find. "No fever. Hmm. How curious." Adam might not be ill, but his smile was certainly sickly.

"Andrew said you was gonna—" Adam's hand clamped over the little girl's mouth, effectively silencing whatever else she was about to say.

"Sleep forever," he finished for her, keeping his hand firmly in place.

Eyes twinkling at the man's discomfort, Meredith couldn't hold back a smile. "I was waiting for my Prince Charming to kiss me awake," she told the little girl.

"Like in *Sleeping Beauty?*" Megan asked wide-eyed, unaware of the peculiar look on her uncle's face at the comment. Of course, she had no way of knowing that Adam hadn't had the privilege of being read to as a child, and didn't know one fairy tale from another.

Allistair Morgan hadn't believed in anything smacking of fantasy or fabrication, and his wife had been forbidden to clutter the children's brains with what he'd perceived as a bunch of nonsensical drivel.

"That's right, squirt. Sleeping Beauty doesn't wake up from the bad witch's spell until the handsome prince comes along and kisses her lips. Must have been some kiss, huh?" She winked at Adam, surprised to find his cheeks ruddy again.

"Is he the prince who used to be a frog?" Andrew wanted to know, despite his aversion to all the mushy talk about kissing. The frog part was okay, though.

Adam leaned forward, fascinated by the tale, hoping the prince, who seemed like an upright sort of guy, hadn't started out life as a ghastly reptile. "Well?" he asked. "Is he?"

Meredith and Megan exchanged knowing looks, then the little girl giggled and rolled her eyes.

"Men!" they said in unison.

MEREDITH ENTERED THE KITCHEN just as Adam hung up the phone. His frown was so lethal, his eyes so cold, it sent shivers of apprehension tap dancing down her spine.

"What is it? What's wrong?" Then it hit her, and she choked on her fear, tears filling her eyes. "Oh, God! It's my mother, isn't it?"

"No. No!" He shook his head. "Forgive me, Meredith. I'm sorry." He drew her into his arms, holding her close, vowing that no one would ever hurt this woman, including him. "It was Peter. He's been trying to reach me since this morning. The battery on my cell phone must be low."

Relief flooded her, and she calmed. "Did he say what was wrong? Nothing serious, I hope." Tired from the trip, she didn't think she could deal with another crisis at the moment.

After dropping the kids off with Mrs. Fishburn, Adam had brought her directly home. She had visions of a hot bath, a cup of cocoa, and sleeping in her own bed. Not even the thought of making love with the handsome millionaire could tempt her tonight.

Taking her hand, he led her into the living room, patting Harrison absently on the head before taking a seat on the sofa. He wondered briefly how Meredith was going to react to what he was about to relate. He didn't want to scare her; she'd been through so much already. But for her own safety she had to be told.

"Curtis Tremayne is in town," he said finally, making her gasp.

"How do you know?"

"He came into your store while you were in Baltimore. Sally spoke with him, then later identified him from a flyer Peter showed her."

"Is Sally all right? Did he hurt her?" Fear for her friend's safety consumed Meredith, and she covered her mouth at the possibility that Sally had suffered at the hands of a madman.

"Sally's fine, love. Tremayne left after finding out you weren't there."

Releasing the breath she'd been holding, her forehead suddenly wrinkled in confusion. "But what does he want with me? I don't even know the man."

Adam caressed her hand, noting how small it looked in his own larger one, how soft and tender it felt, and knowing how vulnerable she would be to a killer like Tremayne. His blood ran cold. "Tremayne hates me as much as I hate him. Maybe more. He obviously knows you and I have been spending a great deal of time together, and has probably put two and two together about our relationship."

"Our relationship? Oh, you mean that we're having an affair?"

Adam recoiled at her choice of words. An affair implied nothing beyond sex. No feelings, no commitment to the relationship. He'd had affairs, and this wasn't one. "We're having much more than an affair, Meredith. At least, I thought we were."

Green eyes widening, she asked, "Oh?"

"We care about each other, and we're going to get married as soon as you stop being so stubborn."

She searched his face, saw the tenderness there, the confusion in his eyes and wondered. "Do you love me, Adam?"

"I'm… I'm not sure." He wouldn't lie. Not about something that important, something that meant so much to her.

It wasn't a no, Meredith thought, taking heart in

the notion. However, it wasn't exactly a qualified yes, either. "Well, when you are sure, then we'll talk about marriage. But until then, we'll just keep things the way they are."

His eyes filled with panic. "But my time's running out, Meredith. I need a wife. The wedding invitations have already been printed for June 21."

"Then I guess you'd better do some soul-searching between now and then. In the meantime, just in case you decide that you're not in love with me, I'll continue interviewing candidates."

With unqualified vehemence, he said, "No. I don't want to see any more videos." He couldn't bear the thought of living his life with someone, anyone, other than Meredith. All women paled in comparison next to his wedding planner.

But was that love?

Damn! Why did this have to be so hard? He conducted successful business dealings every day, made million-dollar decisions that weren't half as difficult. Of course, he'd been dealing with men for the most part. Women weren't nearly as reasonable or sensible. Meredith was living proof of that!

"Would you like to conduct in-person interviews instead? It's your money. You can spend it any way you want."

"What good is money if it can't get me the one thing I truly want."

"Which is?"

"You."

His declaration touched her heart, and she felt a soft fluttering in her chest, but she wouldn't dwell on it. She wouldn't get her hopes up only to have them dashed.

And there were other issues, life-threatening issues, to consider at the moment. "What about Tremayne? Have the police located him yet?" She hoped so. The idea of someone stalking her... She shivered.

The question had him bounding off the couch, and he began to pace the length of the room, clearly agitated. "He's disappeared. But I have a feeling we'll hear from him again. In the meantime, I'd like you to do something for me."

"Of course. Anything."

"I want you to move into my house. You'll be safer there. I can't run the risk of Tremayne finding you alone and unprotected here."

She thought about all those creepy feelings she'd been having lately about someone watching her and wondered if it had been Tremayne. The possibility made Adam's offer all the more tempting, but she couldn't accept it. She couldn't afford to grow more dependent on him than she was already. If the worst happened, the end would be too devastating.

"Anything but that, Adam. I won't move in with you."

Frustration marred his features, and he plowed impatient fingers through his hair. "For God's sake, Meredith! It's not a marriage ploy. I'm trying to protect you from a vicious animal."

"I'll be fine here. I'll call 911 if I see anyone suspicious lurking about. And I have Harrison. Don't forget what a good watchdog he is."

Looking down at the mutt, who had fallen asleep at Meredith's feet, Adam rolled his eyes. "You're going to trust your safety to an oversexed, playful canine?"

Harrison looked up at that moment and bared his teeth in a friendly grin, then fell back to sleep.

"See? He can't even rouse himself to defend my insults. What kind of protector does that make him?"

She patted the dog's head. "Harrison would give his life to protect me, Adam. Never doubt it."

"But he isn't with you all the time. What if Tremayne comes back to your store?"

"Living at your house isn't going to solve that problem. And I do have a business to run, at any rate. Then there's my mother. What reason would I give her for not living at home? I can't tell her the truth. She'd be sick with worry and scared stiff if she thought I was in danger. And that would hardly be good for her recovery."

Pausing before her, he held out his hand, and she went immediately into his arms. "I'll be careful. I promise."

"I could move in here instead," he suggested, knowing from the stubborn set to her chin that she wasn't buying the idea.

"Now how would that look to the folks at social services? You're applying for guardianship. You can't be living with a woman who isn't your wife."

"Well that's your fault."

"And think about the bigger picture, Adam. If we don't go about our lives exactly as we've been doing, Tremayne could get spooked. If you want to catch him, you're going to have to let him play out his hand. It's the only way."

He thought over everything she'd said, then cursed aloud. "You're without a doubt the most exasperating female I've ever met." Covering her mouth with his own, he kissed her with all the passion, tenderness and devotion he possessed, then said when he finally released her, ''I hate it when you're right.''

Meredith caressed his cheek tenderly and smiled. ''Do you think I could have that in writing, Adam? It's so infrequently you admit that I'm right about anything.''

Chapter Sixteen

The weeks flew by with no further sign of Curtis Tremayne. He hadn't tried to contact anyone and hadn't been sighted anywhere in the area.

The police suspected Tremayne's brazen attempt to contact Meredith had been nothing more than a spur-of-the-moment decision, and that he'd probably left West Virginia for good, knowing his risk of discovery was even greater now than before, due to increased police surveillance and the additional private investigators Adam had hired.

Meredith decided that she'd spent enough time worrying about whether or not the man was going to show up on her doorstep. Even Adam had finally conceded that his former brother-in-law wasn't stupid enough to risk capture by showing his face again.

And she had a lot more important things to think about at the moment, like finding Adam Morgan a bride.

A glance at her desk calendar revealed that the millionaire's wedding deadline was fast approaching, and she had yet to find a bridal candidate who met with his approval.

If such a woman even existed.

At this point she had serious doubts. And since he had yet to render any heartfelt declarations of love, she had not accepted any of his continual pleas—make that demands—to marry him.

"What are you going to do, sweetie?" Randall asked, opening the front door to let the June air in. The absence of humidity made the recent warm temperatures delightfully comfortable and most welcome after long dreary months of winter and an unusually wet spring.

Resting her chin on her hands, she heaved a dispirited sigh. "I wish I knew, Randall. Adam and I seem to be at an impasse."

"Even Sally and Peter are talking about marriage, sweetie. Don't you think maybe you should reconsider his—"

She shook her head. "No! I'm happy that Sally has finally allowed herself to love again. And I know she and Peter will be very happy together."

Sally had admitted to Meredith her fears and misgivings about getting involved again so soon. Her track record had not been the best, and she was afraid of making another mistake. But Meredith had sat her down and convinced the frightened woman that Peter wasn't like any of the other men she'd been involved with, that he loved and cherished her, and that Sally was now a totally different person from that needy, insecure woman she used to be.

Apparently her advice had sunk in. At this very moment the happy couple was out shopping for an engagement ring, and Meredith had to admit, if only to herself, that she felt envious of her friend's newfound joy. But as envious as she was, she had no intention of settling for a loveless marriage.

"I'm not going to compromise my beliefs. I can't," she said finally, and her assistant bit back a curse.

Randall hated seeing Meredith so depressed and wished for the hundredth time that the stupid millionaire would come to his senses and tell the anguished woman what she wanted to hear. It was as obvious as the lovesick look he continually wore that Morgan loved Meredith. Why, then, didn't he just tell her so?

Men! Randall thought with no small amount of disgust.

"You've been moping around here for days, sweetie. Even those delectable chocolate éclairs I brought in yesterday from Lovett's weren't enough to put a smile on your face."

The sight of the confections had turned her stomach, but Meredith didn't want to admit that to Randall and risk hurting his feelings. She always felt listless and out of sorts in the spring, though her passion for chocolate did not usually diminish. That, in itself, was rather alarming.

"Okay. I admit it—I've got spring fever. Sometimes it's hard planning weddings for other people, seeing how happy and contented they are, and knowing I'm never going to have a wedding of my own." It was an irony she was finding hard to live with these days.

Perching himself on the edge of her desk, he engulfed her pale hand in his tanned one. "Stop talking like that, or I'll be forced to find you in contempt. *Mon dieu.* You're a beautiful woman, as pretty on the inside as out. Someday it's going to happen for you. I just know it."

"It's already happened. Don't you see, Randall? I'm doomed to live my life like one of those spinsters I read about in romance novels, loving a man who'll never love me back. Never having children." Her eyes filled with tears, and she wiped them away with the back of his hand. Randall stared in horror, trying hard not to scrunch up his nose in distaste.

"I'm sorry for being so maudlin. I must have PMS."

"Now you know perfectly well, sweetie, that Louise is never going to allow you to remain single. She'll take out full-page ads in newspapers, solicit on radio talk shows to find you a man, if necessary. And those heroines you speak of always find happy endings."

Meredith conceded that Randall was right, but it didn't do a thing to boost her spirits.

"By the way, Louise invited me over to Pleasant Acres later this afternoon to play a round of croquet," Randall said. "Her recovery's been remarkable. I can't believe it's the same woman. She's so—" he searched for just the right word "—perky."

Meredith smiled at that. Her mother was the picture of health—rosy cheeks, renewed energy, and interested in things she hadn't cared about in a very long time, like her quilting club and having her hair cut and colored in a becoming style. "Mom's doing great. A few more weeks of recovery and she'll be moving into her own assisted-living apartment at Cedar Springs."

Randall whistled, obviously impressed. "I can't believe you were able to get her in. I hear the waiting list is incredibly long. Must be nice to know people in important places, huh?'' Then he broke into a few bars of ''I've Got Friends in Low Places.''

Meredith couldn't help but smile, even if his Garth Brooks impersonation was absolutely dreadful. She waited until he'd finished, then said, ''Adam sits on the board. He put in a good word for her.'' Another debt of gratitude she owed him.

''Your mother doesn't have a clue that it was Morgan who paid for her transplant, does she?'' He clutched his throat in mock fear. ''I don't want to be around when she finds out.''

Adam was Louise Baxter's savior, and she didn't even know it. One day her mother would have to be told, but not until she was stronger. Meredith was dreading that day. Despite her renewed vigor, Louise hadn't lost any of her animosity toward the Morgans, and she still detested Adam. As unfair as that was, Meredith didn't see her mom changing her attitude anytime soon.

The telephone rang, interrupting her disquieting train of thought. When she answered, Adam's deep voice filled her ear and a thrill of excitement ran through her.

But the thrill quickly dissipated.

''Meredith, have you heard from either Megan or Andrew today?''

The fear in his voice made Meredith's heart begin to pound. ''No. No, I haven't. What's wrong? You sound upset.''

There was an excruciatingly long silence on the other end, then he finally replied, ''I don't want to alarm you, but I think you'd better come over here right away. Both of the kids are missing.''

MEREDITH MADE IT to his house in record time, nearly wrecking her car in the process when she narrowly missed a telephone pole that had jumped out at her from nowhere.

When she burst into Adam's study, it was to find him surrounded by several uniformed police officers and two solemn, official-looking men in suits. Dressed in black, their dark glasses shoved into the front pockets of their jackets, the duo could have been poster boys for the FBI.

She was breathing hard from having run up the front walk, and her words came out in a rush. "I came as soon as I could. Has there been any word?" But she knew from the defeated expression on Adam's face the children had not yet been found.

He shook his head. "Gentlemen, this is Meredith Baxter, a close friend of the family."

She acknowledged the introduction with a forced smile, then picked up her conversation where she'd left off. "When did this happen? Do you suspect it might be Tremayne?"

Latching on to her arm, Adam hauled Meredith out of the room and into the hallway, where they could have some privacy. "It happened a short while ago," he explained. "Mrs. Fishburn picked the kids up from school. They begged her to take them to the park on the way home, and she agreed. While they were playing on the swings, she went to her car to fetch a sweater, and when she returned they were gone."

"Do you suspect Tremayne?" Her stomach twisted at the thought that those innocent children were in the clutches of a deranged lunatic, even if he was their father. "Those poor kids! Megan and Andrew must be scared out of their wits."

And poor Helen Fishburn, she thought. The woman was absolutely crazy in love with those kids. The guilt the housekeeper bore had to be tremendous, though no one blamed her for what happened. Inquiring after the older woman's condition, Meredith was relieved to hear she had been sedated and was resting comfortably upstairs.

Adam slammed his fist against the wall, drawing Meredith's attention back. "It's more than just a suspicion, Meredith. In my gut I know it was Tremayne who took them."

She was surprised by that. "But you led me to believe—"

"I let on that I thought he'd disappeared so you wouldn't continue to worry, but I didn't really believe it. The bastard's got those kids. I know it. And he'll use them against me if he can."

Though she took a deep, calming breath, she was still shaking inside. "What do the police say?"

"Because of the circumstances surrounding the kids' disappearance, the local authorities have brought in the FBI. They're setting up monitoring devices on all of the telephones, in the event he tries to contact us. They may want to monitor your phones at work and home, as well. It's possible Tremayne may try to reach you, since he tried once before."

Meredith felt as though she was in the middle of a Mel Gibson movie, only this wasn't fiction; this was for real. And it scared the heck out of her. There was no telling what Tremayne would do to those kids. He'd killed their mother. Maybe he would—

She bit back the hideous thought, not allowing herself to give up hope. Megan and Andrew were Tremayne's flesh and blood. Surely he had some paternal bond with them, some corner of his heart that was still open to loving them. She had to believe that. She had nothing else to cling to but hope.

"CAN I GET YOU SOME COFFEE?" she asked Adam several hours later. They were seated at the dining room table, half-eaten containers of fast food strewn everywhere. "You hardly touched a bite of your pizza." Not that she could blame him. Hers had tasted like sawdust, and she'd had to fight her nausea all over again. Fortunately, a cola had done wonders to settle her stomach.

"How can I eat, not knowing whether Megan and Andrew have eaten? But, yes, I'd like some coffee. It might help to keep me alert. Special Agent Warrens thinks we may still be contacted tonight."

She filled two ceramic mugs and handed him one. "Tonight? But it's so late. Surely Tremayne would have called by now."

Adam shrugged. "This is my first kidnapping, so I'm not sure what to expect. It's not like in the movies, you know."

"I know," she agreed, squeezing his hand and wishing it were. The movies usually had happy endings.

IT WASN'T UNTIL the following morning that Tremayne made his demands known in the form of a ransom note that had been found by one of the police officers on the windshield of Meredith's car, tucked under one of the wipers, undetected by police surveillance.

The vein in Adam's neck began to throb as he proceeded to read the ransom demands to the group of anxious men and women, who'd set up operations in the house and had dug in for the long haul. Locked up in his world of worry, he seemed oblivious to their presence. Meredith, however, took great comfort in having them there, especially as she listened to the hideous demands:

"Megan and Andrew are unharmed. If you want to see them again, the price is two million dollars to be paid in small, unmarked bills. You'll find the directions to where the money is to be delivered enclosed. Have your wedding planner, Meredith Baxter, make the delivery. She's to come alone. If my instructions are not followed to the letter, you will never see the children again.

Don't be a hero, Morgan. You couldn't save your sister; don't think you can beat me at my own game."

The note wasn't signed, but everyone present knew who it was from, and they all began talking at once.

"That dirty creep! I'll see him in hell," Adam vowed, crumpling the note in his fist before one of the FBI agents secured it in a plastic bag to save as evidence.

Meredith was surprised Tremayne had asked for her involvement. She was surprised and incredibly frightened. She'd never considered herself a braver-than-average person—she was absolutely terrified of spiders—but she intended to do everything within her power to get Megan and Andrew back safely. Even if that included following the instructions of a murderer. The kids' lives could very well depend on her cooperation.

"When do you want me to leave?" she asked, and Adam looked at her as if she were crazy.

"Leave? You're not going anywhere. Do you really think I'd jeopardize your safety, your life, by turning you over to a madman?" He shook his head. "Forget it."

She clutched his arm. "Adam, be reasonable. I'm the only chance Megan and Andrew have. Tremayne may harm them if we don't do what he wants. I don't want that on my conscience. I love those kids too much. And I know you do, too."

"That's true. I love them more than I ever thought possible. But I'm not allowing you to go. And that's final."

Flashing a frustrated look toward Agents Warrens and Fines, who seemed to be taking Adam's refusal in stride, Meredith swore under her breath, then said in a calm voice that belied her exasperation, "If you allow me to make the drop," she ignored the way his eyes widened at the police vernacular, "I'll marry you. It's what you've been wanting. The answer to all of your problems."

Adam didn't waste a moment to consider. "Not even for that," he said, and Meredith knew then and there that he loved her, totally and completely. Her heart lightened, despite the dreadful situation.

"Miss Baxter is correct, Mr. Morgan," Ned Fines said. "She's the best person to make the drop. We can monitor her movements by means of a tracking device, and we'll remain close by to protect her."

"I'd reconsider your position." Agent Warrens added his opinion. "You're dealing with a psychopath. Someone who's totally unpredictable in his behavior. Even though Megan and Andrew are his kids, Tremayne may still harm them. He killed their mother and didn't suffer a bit of remorse over it."

Hoping the men's words had made an impact, Meredith led the reluctant millionaire to the other side of the room, out of earshot from the others. "Please!" she pleaded. "You must reconsider. It's the only way. And I promise to be very careful."

Gazing into eyes as soft and lovely as shamrocks, Adam's throat clogged with trepidation. If anything happened to Meredith, he'd never forgive himself. And he knew in that moment that he loved her, had loved her from the moment he'd first set eyes on her. He loved her more than he'd ever loved anything or anyone. And he wanted to tell her what was in his heart. How much she meant to him. How his world would be destroyed in an instant if she disappeared from it.

But in the end the words wouldn't come, and all he could do was nod his agreement.

"You won't be sorry, Adam. I know this is the best way. The only way," she reassured him.

But as Meredith hurried off to make the necessary arrangements, Adam knew he had never felt such sorrow.

Or such fear.

Chapter Seventeen

Dressed in jeans, a navy T-shirt and a lightweight jacket that Randall had delivered hours earlier, Meredith was about to keep an appointment with the devil.

Driving toward the rendezvous point indicated on Tremayne's sketch, which was located several miles outside of town on a lonely stretch of road, she went over again in her mind the last conversation she'd had with Adam and the FBI agents.

"Are you clear about what it is you have to do, Miss Baxter?" Agent Fines had asked for what seemed like the fiftieth time. The man had looked as nervous as she'd felt, which hadn't buoyed her rapidly sinking self-confidence.

She'd inclined her head. "I think so. I've got the directions right here." She'd held out the paper, then glanced at her watch, her heart jumping to her throat when she'd discovered she had less than an hour to go. She'd been terrified, but she wouldn't let Adam know. She was sure he'd been looking for any excuse to prevent her from carrying out the planned rendezvous.

"I'm to meet Tremayne at the designated spot a

*little after nine, and I'm to keep the tracking device
on my person at all times.''*

"It's in your bra, as we instructed?''

*"Yes,'' she'd replied to Henry Warrens. "And it's
not too comfortable, I can tell you that.''*

*"I'd like to speak to Meredith in private before
she goes.'' The two men had nodded, then everyone
associated with the investigation had disappeared
out of the office.*

*"Come back to me, Meredith. Promise me you
won't do anything stupid, like get yourself killed.''*

She'd hugged him tightly about the waist, pressing
her face into the solid wall of his chest, filling her
nostrils with his musky scent, listening to the rapid
beating of his heart, which mirrored her own. *"I
won't.''* She'd sensed that he'd wanted to tell her
how he felt, but the words were locked deep inside
him. The love he felt for her had been in his eyes, in
his touch, in the sound of his voice, and though he
hadn't said the words, she knew he loved her just
the same.

*"We've got a lot to talk about when I get back,
Mr. Morgan.''* More than she would even admit to
herself at the moment. *"I won't be letting you off the
hook so easily then.''*

She then felt his passionate kiss communicating his
feelings in the only way he knew how.

"It's a date, Miss Baxter.''

Indeed it is, Adam Morgan, and you'd better be
ready to spill your guts when I get back from dropping off this money.

TREMAYNE ADJUSTED THE FOCUS on his binoculars
and spotted the red Mitsubishi as soon as it turned

onto the dirt lane. Morgan had no recourse but to comply with his demands, and his smile was triumphant at knowing the rich guy so well.

He'd been counting on Adam's love for Megan and Andrew, his familial responsibility, Boy Scout character and duty to his beloved dead sister. The poor sap.

Curtis had no intention of hurting the kids. They were his, after all. But, of course, Morgan had no way of knowing that for sure. He also had no intention of taking them along with him when he left. Life on the run would be much easier without two small kids to take care of; he didn't need the brats slowing him down. And with two million in spendable cash at his disposal, he'd be able to go just about anywhere his heart desired and resume the kind of life he'd grown so accustomed to while he'd been married to Allison.

Morgan's sexy delivery girl was just frosting on the cake as far as he was concerned, and he intended to have a taste. What better way to get back at Morgan than to take something he wanted?

MEREDITH SPOTTED the sports utility vehicle as soon as she turned down the dirt road and had gone about a mile. It was dark and deserted out here in the middle of nowhere. The wind blew just enough to add an eerie feel to the already spooky scenario, and ripples of fear coursed down her spine, which was already damp with perspiration.

She touched the tracking device secured to her bra just to make sure it was in place, to make her feel not quite so alone, then muttered another prayer, figuring it couldn't hurt. Her heart was pounding so hard in her chest she could hear it in her ears. Her hands were sweating so profusely, even the leather grip of the steering wheel didn't help.

As she got closer, the headlights illuminated Megan and Andrew standing beside their father's car, and she breathed a sigh of relief that they appeared to be unharmed. They looked small and absolutely terrified, which gave her the courage to do what she had to do. Tremayne stood behind them, his hands resting on their shoulders, an implied warning that they shouldn't think about running away.

"Here goes nothing," she muttered, her palm slipping on the metal door handle as she tried to open it. Stepping out of her car, she thought about Adam, about the fact that she might never see him again, and as her heart grew heavy, she grew more determined.

Pushing her fears aside, Meredith held up the large black canvas bag containing the money. It had taken Adam several hours to get it together, but he'd managed with Peter's help to secure the required funds. The two million dollars now rested in her hands.

"I've got your money, Mr. Tremayne," she called out. "Now let the children go." She tried to sound confident, in charge, but her knees were knocking so badly she was sure he could tell she was scared.

"I want to see the money first. Drop the bag and move away from the car where I can see you." He approached cautiously, but the kids remained rooted to the spot, as they'd been instructed. Curtis had threatened to kill their friend Meredith if they so much as moved a muscle.

The frightened woman did as instructed, and Curtis inched closer, the knife he held ready to be used without a moment's hesitation in the event she hadn't come alone. "At last we meet, Miss Baxter," he said with a practiced smile. "Sorry it had to be under such unfortunate circumstances."

She took a deep breath, wondering how monsters could look so normal. "You've got your money. Now release the kids so I can take them home where they belong."

He looked around to make sure the area was secure. "Did you come alone? How very brave of you."

"I'm alone." The FBI was supposedly tracking her from a discreet distance, but she hadn't seen any sign of them since leaving the Morgan residence. They were reputed to be good at this sort of thing. She hoped caution was the only reason they hadn't made their presence known.

"I'm not dumb enough to think you're not being tracked or followed, Miss Baxter. So, unless you'd like me to do a thorough search of your more private areas, I suggest you remove whatever clever device the FBI has provided."

In the beam of the headlight she saw the flicker of metal and realized he was holding a knife. She choked back a scream. Megan and Andrew were watching her, their eyes wide with fright, and she tried to brazen it out. "I don't know what you mean, Mr. Tremayne."

Before she could anticipate his reaction, he stepped forward and grabbed her arm. "I think you do, Meredith. Now, unless you want me to cut off every inch of your clothing—something I'd be more than happy to do—you'll tell me where the device is hidden."

"Tell him, Meredith!" Andrew called out, his voice frantic and pleading.

Realizing she'd been outsmarted, Meredith finally relented. "It's in my bra," she admitted, knowing she'd just given up any hope of being rescued.

He arched a brow, then gave her a sadistic smile. "Really? Shall I retrieve it, or will you?"

Turning away from him, though he still gripped one arm tightly, she reached under her shirt and removed the tiny tracking device, bringing it forth to show him.

"Very sensible of you, Meredith. Now toss it into the car, and we'll be on our way."

Her eyes widened in fear. "But you said all you wanted was the money."

"I lied. I've decided that traveling alone is a drag. I think it'd be a lot more fun if I were to take you along." She made as if to bolt, but he tightened his hold. "I wouldn't do anything stupid if you have any feelings at all for those kids. I'd hate for them to see another murder victim."

"You disgust me," she said.

He shrugged. "Sometimes I disgust myself, but that's not really here nor there. Now get in my car and be quick about it. I want to put some distance between you and your friends. They should be arriving shortly, unless they discovered upon leaving Morgan's house that their vehicles had been tampered with." His eyes shone triumphant.

"You bastard!"

"Tsk, tsk. Such language in front of the children. My dead wife would have been horrified. Allison never swore in front of Megan and Andrew. But then, she wasn't filled with passion, as you seem to be. I'm a great admirer of passion." His gaze roamed every inch of her, making her skin crawl, and it was all she could do not to scream.

"Adam will kill you for this."

He laughed. "I doubt it. He's not that kind of man, doesn't have the stomach for it. All that money's made him soft. Besides, as I'm sure you've already learned, he's not a man who forms attachments. He likes his life uncomplicated."

"You don't know him at all," she flung at him.

"It's not Adam I want to know, Meredith. It's you."

BACK AT THE MORGAN RESIDENCE, Adam was pacing back and forth in the driveway like a caged animal. "Dammit, Warrens! How could you let this happen?" He stared daggers at the FBI agent, who was in turn staring under the hood of his van and shaking his head in dismay.

"I underestimated Tremayne. But don't worry. This is only a minor setback. We'll catch up to Miss Baxter."

"My car's been tampered with, too," Fines called out. "And so has Mr. Morgan's."

Glancing at his watch, Adam knew real fear for the first time in his life. "Meredith left over fifteen minutes ago. How do you propose to catch up with her, now that you've given her such a healthy head start?"

"The tracking device, remember?" Warrens replied confidently, then flipped on the small computerized screen in his van and fiddled with the controls. "I'm not picking up anything," he admitted over his shoulder.

Fisting his hands before he struck the older man, Adam let loose with a colorful epithet. "Why doesn't that surprise me? Dammit, man! Do something. The woman I love is soon to be in the hands of a murderer." The admission surprised him. He hadn't voiced his feelings for Meredith until now. It made it seem real. He knew it felt right.

Adam wasn't a praying man, but he prayed to the Almighty that Meredith and the children's lives would be spared. He prayed harder than he'd ever prayed before.

"Fines, call in and get a helicopter to pick us up," Warrens ordered. "And tell them to be quick about it. Miss Baxter is out there on her own."

ALONE WITH THE KIDS in what appeared to be a deserted mine shaft, Meredith comforted Megan and Andrew as best she could, trying to think of a way out of her present predicament. Tremayne had locked them in a roughly constructed storage area and had taken the key to the padlock when he'd left.

He'd gone to make arrangements for their departure, that much she knew. And he intended to carry out his threat of taking her with him. His intentions had been made disgustingly clear after consuming over half a bottle of whisky he'd had stored in the mine, along with some other provisions. Apparently he'd been living in the mine for several weeks. It reeked of old campfires.

Their only chance to survive would be to escape before he returned. She didn't want to think about the consequences if they didn't. A man such as he, who had killed a woman, would have no compunction about murdering another.

Frantically searching her pockets for something she could use to pick the lock, which held the chicken-wire door closed, she came up empty-handed. "Think! Think! What else? What else can I use?"

"Are we going to die in here, Meredith?" Megan asked, snuggling closer to her side.

She tried to comfort the frightened child. "No, sweetie," she said, patting her cheek. "I promise we're going to be all right. I just need to find something we can use to pick the lock."

"I've searched through my dad's stuff, Meredith, and I didn't find nothing," Andrew informed her when he returned from his hunt.

Suddenly, as if God had provided a sign, her gaze landed upon Megan's shiny silver hair barrettes. "Thank you," she whispered, then said to the little girl, "I need your barrettes, sweetie. I'm going to use them to pick the lock." She'd seen it done in a movie once and hoped it wasn't just some bit of movie magic a clever script writer had dreamed up.

The child pulled the items from her hair and handed them to Meredith, smiling tentatively. "Murphy thinks it'll work."

"Me, too," she said with a wink.

"Me, three," Andrew added, his voice shaking, though he was trying very hard to be brave.

The padlock was old and rusted. Meredith reached her fingers through the chicken-wire covered door frame to grasp the lock, inserting the tip of the barrette into it. Jiggling it back and forth, she prayed all the while that her efforts would work. "Don't fail me now, God. You're going to make me look bad." A few more twists and turns of the barrette and the lock sprung open. "Yes!" she screeched. "We did it."

With Andrew and Megan's help, she pushed open the door and, grabbing their hands, ran for all she was worth, out of the mine and into the blackness of the night.

When they came upon the dirt road, Meredith headed in the direction she thought her car was parked, using the glow of the city's lights to guide her. Suddenly she heard a strange whirring noise in the distance.

Excitement filled her, along with hope. "I think it's a helicopter," she told the kids.

"Do you think Uncle Adam's on it?"

"I don't know, Megan. We'll just have to wait and see. I hope so."

"Look!" Andrew pointed down the road toward the approaching headlights, his face contorting in fear. "That must be my dad. He's gonna be really mad when he finds out we left the mine. He might kill us, like he killed my mom."

The child's point was well taken. "Quick! Drop down on your tummies and be very quiet. It's dark, the weeds are tall, and he won't be able to see us behind this outcropping of rocks."

They did as instructed, hardly breathing as they watched the SUV pass them by. When it had gone, they let out a collective breath.

"Let's go," Meredith directed, and they ran toward the noise in the sky. Finally spotting the helicopter, they waved their arms frantically in the air, shouting, "Down here! Down here!"

"Look," Adam said, pointing toward the ground. "Shine your light down there. I see movement." The light illuminated Meredith, Megan and Andrew running toward them, but Adam's relief was short-lived as he spotted Tremayne's vehicle in hot pursuit.

"Put down, put down. Tremayne's spotted them."

"It's too rocky," the pilot said. "I'm not sure—"

"Then lower me down on a rope, dammit! I'm not going to watch that murderer kill the three people who mean the most to me."

"Do as he says," Warrens ordered. "We'll set down on the road and be right behind you."

"Yeah, right," Adam said with a healthy amount of skepticism, latching on to the heavy metal cable and wondering if he had the skill to pull this off. He knew he had the motivation.

"It's Uncle Adam," Andrew said, pointing at the man who was dangling from the cable that was slowly being lowered to the ground. "He's coming to save us."

Meredith's gaze followed the small boy's, and her eyes widened in disbelief. Dressed to the nines in his Armani suit and wingtips, Adam was coming to their rescue.

You had to love a man who had that much style, she thought.

"Megan! Andrew!"

Tremayne's voice filled the night air, and Meredith looked back to see he had abandoned his car and was fast approaching on foot. "Hurry, Adam!" she screamed, then realized what she was saying. The man had a knife, and he'd kill Adam if he got the chance.

"Come on, kids," she urged. "We've got to run faster. We can't let your father catch us."

"But my side hurts, Meredith," Megan complained in a breathless voice. "And Murphy's tired, too."

"Tell Murphy he can have all the ice cream, cake and cookies he can eat for a whole week if he keeps up."

"He said okay." Meredith couldn't help but smile at the child, despite their precarious predicament. Bribery was so very effective with children, she mused, ignoring the stitch in her side.

"Come back here, you bitch!" Tremayne was gaining on them, but Meredith didn't dare look back. If she had, she would have noticed that Adam was now behind them, as well. He'd let go of the rope and was at this very moment giving new meaning to the words "flying tackle."

"You murderer!" he shouted at Tremayne, punching the fugitive in the face with a hard blow after he'd landed on top of him. The sound of crunching bone was music to his ears. "That was for Allison." Then he hit him again and again, his fury giving him strength he didn't know he possessed. "And for Meredith, Megan and Andrew," he added.

Despite the vicious blows Adam delivered, Tremayne was strong and fought back, landing several punches of his own. "You blue-blooded rich boy! You've never known what it is to go without, to be on the outside looking in," Curtis shouted back. "All your life you've had everything you ever wanted, while I had to settle for the leavings."

"Settle for this, you bastard," Adam said, shoving

a fist into his mouth to shut him up. Blood spurted everywhere, as did a couple of Tremayne's teeth.

The two men scrambled on the ground, rolling over and over; the sound of knuckles and fists scraping skin, bones cracking like dried twigs, and blood-curdling screams filled the night air. Until finally there was silence.

"What's happening? I can't see," Andrew said, jumping up and down, trying to get a better look.

"I can't say for certain, but I think your Uncle Adam has beaten your father to a pulp." She tried to contain her grin, not knowing how Megan and Andrew would respond.

The kids took a moment to consider this, then let loose with a cheer.

The FBI arrived and took matters into their own hands. Tremayne's limp body was handcuffed and hauled to a waiting ambulance.

"I'm sorry about the problems tonight, Miss Baxter," Agent Warrens said when everything was finally under control. "Sometimes things don't go as smoothly as we'd like."

His apology fell on deaf ears as Meredith ran toward Adam. He was bloodied and disheveled, and sporting a whopper of a black eye, but she'd never seen anything or anyone more beautiful in her life. "Adam," she said, throwing her arms about him and hugging him close. He grunted when his bruised ribs protested. "I was so worried Tremayne was going to kill you. He had a knife."

Adam hadn't even considered his own life. All he could think about was Tremayne putting his hands on Meredith and the kids, and that had made him wild. If the FBI hadn't shown up when they did, he wasn't sure what he might have done. He'd never hurt another human being before, but then, he'd never felt so angry and out of control before. And he'd never hated anyone the way he hated Curtis Tremayne.

Kissing the top of her head, he winced. His lower lip was cut and swollen to twice its normal size. "If I'd known that, I might not have been so impulsive," he lied.

"Oh, Adam, please promise me you'll never again do anything so brave or foolish. I died a thousand deaths watching you dangle from that cable."

"But, love, the heroes in your romance novels always rescue their ladies. How could I do any less?"

Her eyes widened as his words sunk in, and she took a step back and looked up at him. "You read a romance novel?"

His grin was lopsidedly wonderful. "Several, actually. I liked them. Especially the sexy—"

"Stop! The children are coming."

"Uncle Adam! Uncle Adam!" Megan and Andrew cried out in unison, wrapping their arms around his legs. "You were just like Arnold Schwarzenegger," Andrew said proudly. "You really kicked butt!"

Meredith and Adam exchanged amused looks, then Adam, who had recently viewed one of the actor's films with his nephew said, "Let's go home. This terminator has had enough excitement for one night."

Chapter Eighteen

The morning after the longest night Meredith had ever spent, she was back at work at the bridal boutique. Despite Adam's suggestion—make that *demand*—that she take a few days off to recover from her ordeal, she'd decided that returning to her normal routine was the very best stress-reducing therapy she could think of.

And she needed time to get a few things in order before keeping her scheduled dinner appointment with Adam this evening.

He had informed her after driving her home early this morning that he intended to cancel his wedding plans and would take his chances with the court on his own. But she had convinced him, after much wheedling and cajoling, that she had found the perfect bridal candidate, and that it would be rude and inconsiderate of him not to allow her to present the woman, after all the hard work she'd done on his behalf. He had finally relented, though he had made it very clear that there wasn't anyone she could present who would change his mind on the subject.

We'll just see about that, Mr. Morgan.

Sally strolled into the store wearing a big smile

and an even bigger engagement ring. Rushing forward, she gave Meredith a hug. "When Peter finally told me what was happening, I was frantic with worry. Are you all right?"

"I'm fine. Tremayne's in jail, the kids are scheduled to see a therapist, though they seem perfectly fine to me, just a bit shaken up, and I've been too busy making decisions to dwell on what happened. I'm looking ahead to the future."

Taking a seat at the table, Sally poured herself a cup of coffee, refilling Meredith's cup as well. "Well, you're a far stronger woman than I am, Meredith, so I'm not at all surprised by your attitude. I would have probably fallen apart."

Meredith reached out to pat her friend's hand. "Posh! You would have done just fine. To tell you the truth I was more stupid than brave. And scared to death the entire time. I'm just glad the kids are safe and that Tremayne will spend the rest of his life in prison." With no possibility of parole, if the D.A. had his way.

"You said on the phone you had something important you wanted to discuss with me. You know I'm happy and quite willing to do anything I can to help. So, if you need to take some extra time off, I'll fill in for you. After what you've just been through, I can certainly understand why you'd need to."

"I may just do that, Sally, and thank you, but that's not entirely the reason I asked you to come in early today. I have a proposition for you that I hope you're going to like."

"A proposition? Now that does sound intriguing."

"I want to make you a partner in Best Laid Plans."

"A partner?" Brown eyes rounded in surprise. "I'm sorry to sound like a parrot, but—I don't understand. This is your business, which you've worked very hard to make successful. Why would you want a partner?"

"Because I'm planning to take on another role, and I'm going to need more time to devote to it."

"You are?"

Meredith nodded. "Are you interested? If not, I can ask Randall, though I know his heart is set on becoming a corporate attorney. He's already been offered a position in a firm located in the middle of New York's garment district. Just think, he'll be close to all the designer clothes, and he'll actually be able to afford them after passing the bar."

Sally grinned. "I'm so happy for him. And yes, I'm definitely interested in your offer. As you know, Peter and I plan to be married in the fall, but we've decided to wait awhile before having children." Her expression grew thoughtful, and she chewed her lower lip. "I'm afraid I don't have much money put aside to invest. How much were you thinking of asking?"

As Meredith thought about the plan she intended to put into action, a mischievous smile crossed her face. Last night's brush with death had convinced her that time and life were too precious too waste. "It isn't your money I need, Sally, but your expertise with the video camera."

"The video—" The woman's mouth unhinged as the import of Meredith's words sank in. "No! You're not going to—"

"Oh, but I am."

ADAM PACED BACK AND FORTH in front of the blank television screen, agitated by Meredith's decision and his own foolish agreement that she could show him another bridal candidate video.

He had absolutely no intention of marrying anyone other than Meredith and had finally gotten up his nerve to bare his soul and confess his feelings for her. Only now he had to postpone his declaration, and it was making him a nervous wreck.

Meredith's voice was laced with impatience, when she said, "Adam, will you please sit down and watch this video with me? You promised you would, and after everything I've been through, the least you can do is humor me."

"But we need to talk." Didn't she know how hard this was for him? Didn't she know that he had practiced in front of the mirror at least a hundred times what he was going to say and how he was going to say it? It had to be perfect. Romantic. The most brilliant declaration of love and a wedding proposal that had ever been delivered. It had to be the stuff of poets and romance novels. Meredith would expect no less.

Noting his frustration, she could only imagine the turmoil going on inside him. Turmoil that was likely to be increased quite soon. She patted the space next to her. "We'll talk for as long as you like, *after* you've watched this video. I promise."

Casting her a look of unadulterated frustration, he plopped down on the couch next to her. "Did I tell you how lovely you look tonight?"

She kissed him quickly and carefully on the mouth, since his lips were still a bit swollen. "At least five times. Now be quiet and watch. And hand me some popcorn, will you?'' This was a heck of a time for Adam to turn into a chatterbox, she thought, clicking on the VCR.

The videotape began. Sally's voice could be heard in the background asking the first question, then the camera zoomed in on the applicant, who was seated demurely, hands folded in her lap. ''Please state your name and occupation for the camera.''

''Meredith Baxter, owner of Best Laid Plans.''

''What?'' Adam asked, clearly confused.

''What is your reason for wanting to marry Adam Morgan, Miss Baxter?''

Adam's gasp was audible as he watched Meredith smile directly into the camera, his eyes glued to the screen.

''Well, other than the fact that he has the most adorable tush and is beyond heroic—'' Sally giggled in the background ''—I love him to distraction, and I want to spend the rest of my life with him, in and out of bed.''

Staring openmouthed at the television, then at Meredith, who was grinning at him from ear to ear, he asked, ''You made a video? You want to marry me?''

''Yes, I want to marry you, Adam Morgan. I'm totally and shamelessly in love with you.''

A grin spreading over his face, he hugged her to his chest, kissing every inch of her face. ''I love you, too. I...I was just too stupid to realize it.''

She caressed his cheek. ''I know, Adam. And I forgive you for your denseness.''

''You do? And you're going to marry me? Meredith, I love you so much it hurts.''

She wouldn't speculate where he was hurting, but

there was a definite bulge in his— "To show you how much I love you," she said quickly, trying to refocus her attention on the matter at hand, "I've brought you a present."

"But you shouldn't have. I don't have anything for you." He didn't know declarations were supposed to be accompanied by gifts. He must have skimmed over that scene.

"Oh, but, Adam, you've already given me the most precious gift a man can give a woman."

"I have?" His smile became self-consciously sweet, and Meredith's heart felt full to bursting. "Oh, you mean love."

Reaching into her purse, she extracted a small, white plastic object, placing it in his hand. "Well, there is that, of course. But I was talking about this little pink plus sign—a sign of our enthusiastic and unprotected lovemaking sessions."

He stared at the wand, at the radiant glow on her face, and then her words finally sank in. "You're going to have a baby?"

Taking his hand, she placed it on her abdomen. "We're going to have a baby, Adam. You and me. And it'll probably be the first of many, if my mother has anything to say about it." Which she would, Meredith was certain.

Adam couldn't have looked more stunned if he'd been poleaxed, and Meredith knew a moment of concern, then he let loose with a very un-Adamlike whoop of joy, kissed her until her toes curled heavenward, and said, almost as an afterthought, "But your mother hates me."

"Yes, well, there is that. But she'll come around. Especially when she learns you're so fertile. Louise

Baxter wants grandchildren. And she'll accept even you as a son-in-law to get them.''

"That's comforting," he said with a grin, then kissed her again. "I think we should go upstairs and celebrate our engagement. I mean, it's not every day a man learns he's going to be married and have a child.''

She pretended to think about it. "Well, I guess we could go upstairs, uncork a bottle of club soda and make use of that big marble tub to see how long you can hold your breath under water."

Scooping her up in his arms, he flashed her a wildly erotic grin. "I've got generations of coal miner's genes flowing through me, love. I can stay submerged for a very long time."

Meredith's eyes widened. "Oh, my!"

"Exactly."

There's more to the Morgan saga than
Adam and Meredith. Get the whole story
from the beginning in
Harlequin Historicals

THE MARRYING MAN

by

Millie Criswell

Available April 2000

Chapter One

Autumn 1888, Morgantown, West Virginia

"You need a wife, Ash, and there ain't no getting around that fact."

With his ladderback chair propped up against the exterior wall of the stone house, the dark-haired man swallowed a healthy dose of sourmash whisky, screwing his face up in disgust, a clear indication of his feelings on the subject of matrimony.

The sun had just dipped into the horizon, streaking the autumn sky a reddish-gray color. In another hour it would be too cold to sit outside, so Ash intended to enjoy what time he had left. He'd spent too many hours underground in the coal mines not to cherish breathing fresh mountain air and wide-open spaces.

It was obvious his uncle expected him to comment, so he obliged the old man by saying, "I've had me two wives, Uncle Zeke. And that's about all a man should have to suffer in one lifetime."

The old man nodded and puffed on his pipe. "That may be true, boy. Being a bachelor, I've never been overly fond of the whole marrying institution myself. But you got a child to think of.

"Addy's growing up wild with no woman around to tell her right from wrong. She looks like a boy most of the time, with her hair chopped off at crazy angles." The child had taken scissors to her long, brown locks, claiming her hair always got in the way when she was climbing trees and scampering over rocks. Ash hadn't bothered to take her to task for it, saying it was her hair and she had a right to cut it if she wanted. The boy was too permissive, in Zeke's opinion.

"That child smells worse than bear droppings downwind, 'cause she don't bathe regularlike, Ash, and I'm telling you that it's time you up and married again. For the girl's sake."

Ashby Morgan's silver eyes narrowed as he continued to gaze at his uncle. Zeke was a well-meaning man, and Ash loved the old geezer like a father, but he didn't hold with any man telling him how to live his life or raise his daughter. He and Addy had been doing just fine these past eleven years on their own. And even if she was a bit of a tomboy, who was to say that was wrong? In time she'd grow out of it.

"You don't bathe regularly, either, old man," Ash pointed out, "so you got no call to talk that way about Addy." The old man harrumped, tapping his pipe on the sole of his mud-caked boot to empty the ashes, then opened his mouth to say something else, but Ash continued, not allowing him to interrupt.

"And you know damn well that it's a woman's role in life to change a man. Adelaide tried it, and before her, Wynona. I loved them both, God rest their souls, but I'm not sorry to have my freedom. I didn't ask the Almighty to take them from me like he did, but I took it as a sign that he wanted me to remain a single man."

Ezekiel Allistair Morgan pulled on his chin whiskers, as was his habit when he was frustrated or agitated about something. Ash had always been headstrong, even as a child, and it wasn't hard to tell where his daughter inherited her contrary disposition from. The stubborn young boy had grown into a stubborn fool-of-a-man; young Addy, it seemed, was destined to follow in his footsteps.

All the Morgan men, himself included, suffered from thick-headedness, as his mama used to say. Ash's father, Aaron, had been particularly afflicted with the problem, which is why he'd failed to live beyond his thirtieth birthday. Morgan men had certain traits that couldn't be denied—the silvery-gray eyes for one thing, the stubbornness for another.

"What about a few years from now when the men start to call? Addy's starting to grow up. In case you ain't noticed, boy, she's sprouting bosoms," he said, making Ash's eyes widen. "Don't you wanna get that girl married and off your hands? No man's gonna look twice in her direction, unless you get her whipped into shape. She's behind in her learning, and she sure as heck ain't had no refinements. You got to admit—you ain't set much of an example by her."

The younger man's face suffused with guilt, and Zeke took it as a sign of capitulation, plunging ahead into uncharted waters. "I know you only want what's best for the girl. We all do. You know I love that child to death, and would do anything for her. Which is why I've taken it upon myself to put a plan into motion."

"What?" The younger's man's eyes filled with suspicion, and he frowned, rocking forward, the chair legs hitting the porch floorboards with a thud. "What have you done, old man? Don't tell me you've been playing matchmaker again, because I won't stand for it, Uncle Zeke. I told you none of the women in this town interest me." Attending to the daily operations of the coal mine didn't leave much time to devote to romancing a woman, anyway. Not that Ash was the least bit inclined. His needs could be satisfied at O'Connor's House of Pleasure when his urges got too strong to be denied.

Zeke's eyes, a shade darker than his nephew's, lit with a steely glint of determination and just a hint of satisfaction. "I figured as much, boy, which is why I took it upon myself to write this here lady." Removing a wrinkled newspaper advertisement from his back pocket, he smoothed it out and handed it to Ash, whose frown was deepening by the moment.

"Miss Dorothea Cartwright runs one of them finishing schools in Philadelphia—The Cartwright School of Finishing and Comportment. A real high-falutin sort of establishment from the sounds of it."

His gaze drifting to the plump cardinal lighting on the spindly branch of the sycamore gracing the front yard, Ash's frown smoothed somewhat. "And you want me to send Addy to this woman?" he asked, rubbing his chin, as if considering the idea, which admittedly had some merit. "I don't know..."

Zeke shook his head. "That weren't my thinking. Leastways, it wouldn't be right to do that, since you promised Adelaide on her deathbed that you'd always keep young Addy by your side."

"Yeah, I did." Ash's forehead wrinkled in confusion. "So why'd you write this woman then?" Suddenly a mischievous smile lifted the corners of his mouth. "You been carrying on some kind of romantic correspondence with Miss Cartwright behind the widow's back, you sly old dog?" His full-fledged grin made Zeke snort contemptuously.

"Very funny. It just so happens that Miss Cartwright teaches girls to become ladies. That's what a finishing school does. I asked Etta about it." The widow Dobbins, as she was known around Morgantown, was the love of Ezekiel Morgan's life, though the old man would rather die than admit that to anyone, especially his nephew, whom he knew would tease him unmercifully if he learned just how sweet Zeke was on the widow.

"I wrote Miss Cartwright and told her that you was needin' a wife and a mother for your young daughter, and asked her if she could recommend one of her girls for the job. Her girls are all refined types from good families. It says so right here, so I thought—"

"You what?" Ash bolted from his chair, shoving his furious face into his uncle's startled one. Zeke, who'd been leaning casually against the porch rail up until then, had now straightened and was ready for flight, just in case. Ashby Morgan had a mean temper when pushed, and Zeke may have pushed a tad too far.

"Are you crazy, Uncle Zeke? Do you actually think I'm stupid enough to marry some woman I've never met?" His eyes flashed quicksilver, and he shook his head. "That's not going to happen, so write the woman back and tell her to forget it."

His weathered face paling considerably, Zeke decided to put some distance between himself and his nephew, and he moved around the angry man. Not that Ash would ever hit him, but a man couldn't be too careful. Zeke didn't have that many teeth left, but what he had, he intended to keep.

"It's...it's too late for that, boy. I already got a reply from Miss Cartwright. Said she was sending a young woman by the name of Sarah Jane Parker. Claims she fits the bill and will make you a wonderful wife. And," he added to emphasize his point, "an excellent mother for Addy."

"Well, write her back and tell her the deal's off. I'm not in the market for a bride, mail-order or otherwise."

"Can't. Already sent the train fare with my first letter, so there's nothing to keep her from coming. She'll be here any day now. The train from Philadelphia's due in to Fairmont day after tomorrow."

Ash's pulse began throbbing like a bubbling geyser, and the younger man let loose a string of curses, his fists clenched tightly at his side, as if the idea of striking out had crossed his mind. "I can't believe this!" He kicked the chair and sent it flying off the porch, and the older man's eyes widened a fraction, but he held his ground.

"I did what I though was best for you and Addy," Zeke tried to explain. "I promised your daddy I'd take care of you when he went off to that damn war back in '61 and got hisself blowed up clear to kingdom come. I've tried to do right by you these many years." He squeezed Ash's shoulder, relieved when the angry man didn't pull away. Zeke loved the boy as if he'd sprung from his own loins.

"Morgan Coal Mining is taking off, Ash. Soon

most all your time's gonna be spent at the mine. And if you expand your holdings, like we talked about, then you'll have even less time to devote to Addy's upbringing.

"You need a wife, boy. You don't have to love her. You don't even have to like her. You just got to marry her and let her be a mother to your girl."

The idea of living life with a woman from Philadelphia filled Ash with distaste. No doubt Miss Parker was some white-gloved, snooty society type. The kind of woman who ate an orange with a knife and fork instead of digging right into the meat of it—someone who quoted Bible scripture every chance she got, probably right before bedtime.

Life in the mountains was arduous. The work was hard, the winters harsh; he needed a helpmate, not a hindrance. "Miss Parker's a city girl, Zeke. She'll never fit in here."

"Your mama was a city girl through and through, boy, and she adjusted to life here in the mountains just fine. I'm not saying it's gonna be easy for her. But if Sarah Jane Parker's got smarts, which the letter claims she does, and gumption, which I hope she will, then she'll fare all right. You've got to give her a chance."

"She may be repulsed by my looks," the younger man said hopefully, trying a different tack, and was disappointed when Zeke threw back his head and laughed at the absurdity of the notion.

"It's embarrassing going into town with you and watching the way them women throw themselves in your path. They're like bitches in heat, and you don't pay them no nevermind. I ain't worried in the least about Miss Parker finding you to her liking."

"What if she looks like the hind end of a mule?"
Not that he was planning to sleep with her, but still…
A chill ran down his spine.

Reaching into his back pocket once again, the old
man extracted a photograph and handed it to his
nephew, a pleased-as-punch smile lighting a face
mapped with lines of age and wisdom. "She ain't no
mule, boy. She's a Thoroughbred, if this picture can
be believed."

Studying the likeness, Ash's eyes widened in surprise. Miss Sarah Jane Parker was fair-skinned, and
possessed two deep-set dimples in her cheeks. Her
nose was small and slightly upturned, and she had
the devil's own twinkle in her eyes.

"She's a looker, I'll give you that. But she seems
a mite young to be taking on the responsibilities of
a wife and mother." She couldn't be more than nine-
teen or twenty, hardly much older than his daughter,
and a full ten years younger than himself.

"The younger the better, I always say. She'll be
like a young filly. You can break her in just the way
you like before riding her." The old man chuckled.
"She won't be set in her ways or prone to give you
any trouble, like the last Mrs. Morgan." Zeke puckered his mouth disapprovingly at the memory of
Ash's late wife, who'd had an opinion on just about
every little thing and had driven Zeke nuts with her
constant jabbering.

"A docile young woman is sure to make an excellent wife," he concluded.

Ash considered his uncle's words, then finally
smiled. He was beginning to warm to the idea of a
docile wife who'd say, "Yes, Ash. Of course, Ash.

You're right, Ash.'' Neither of his first two wives had been all that easy to get along with.

Wynona'd been only sixteen when they'd married, and she hadn't wanted children. She'd been resistant to bed him, fearing she'd end up pregnant and die in childbirth like her mother. Having his way with her had been a constant battle, up until the day she fell into the Monongahela River and drowned, six months after their wedding.

Adelaide had been an earthy woman who liked the marriage bed, but she'd been too damn opinionated about everything. Her daddy had been a coal miner down in Kentucky, and she thought she knew everything there was to know about the mining business.

She and Zeke had bickered about everything having to do with the mine. The old man had pulled no punches about his belief that a woman had no business in a man's domain, and Ash had been inclined to agree with him.

If Adelaide hadn't died in childbirth, Ash wasn't sure they'd have stayed married. A talkative, opinionated woman did wear on a man's nerves.

Sarah Jane Parker was supposedly docile. He liked that.

Docile. Refined. And no doubt spiritless.

She sounded almost perfect.

And that's what worried him. Ash had never met a perfect woman. He doubted there was such a thing.

So he made up his mind right then and there that if Sarah Jane Parker proved even the least bit difficult or opinionated he'd send her packing before she could untangle her corset strings.

HEART OF THE WEST

Every Man Has His Price!

Lost Springs Ranch was famous for turning young mavericks into good men. So word that the ranch was in financial trouble sent a herd of loyal bachelors stampeding back to Wyoming to put themselves on the auction block!

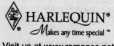

HARLEQUIN®
Makes any time special ™

Visit us at www.romance.net

PHHOWGEN

Coming in January 2000
Classics for two of your favorite series.

SECRET VOWS by **REBECCA YORK** & **KELSEY ROBERTS**

From the best of Rebecca York's

43 Light St.

Till Death Us Do Part

Marissa Devereaux discovered that paradise wasn't all it was cracked up to be when she was abducted by extremists on the Caribbean island of Costa Verde.... But things only got worse when Jed Prentiss showed up, claiming to be her fiancé.

From the best of Kelsey Roberts's

THE ROSE TATTOO

Unlawfully Wedded

J.D. was used to getting what he wanted from people, and he swore he'd use that skill to hunt down Tory's father's killer. But J.D. wanted much more than gratitude from his sassy blond bride—and he wasn't going to clue her in. She'd find out soon enough...if she survived to hear about it.

Available January 2000 at your favorite retail outlet.

HARLEQUIN®
Makes any time special ™